T0368748

In The Fringe has had multiple editors comb its pages. However, various errors in grammar and punctuation remain within the context of the story in order to preserve its authentic narrative style.

Written for *that girl* who dares to acknowledge the walls, corners and ceiling in her life.

in
the fringe

by
Eleanor Summers

Order this book online at www.trafford.com
or email orders@trafford.com

Most Trafford titles are also available at major online book retailers.

Printed in the United States of America.

ISBN: 978-1-4251-0231-9 (soft)
ISBN: 978-1-4251-9364-5 (ebook)

*Our mission is to efficiently provide the world's finest, most comprehensive book publishing
service, enabling every author to experience success. To find out how to publish your
book, your way, and have it available worldwide, visit us online at www.trafford.com*

Trafford rev. 8/12/2010

 www.trafford.com

North America & international
toll-free: 1 888 232 4444 (USA & Canada)
phone: 250 383 6864 ♦ fax: 812 355 4082

Introduction To The Fringe

This is a story of a girl. It is a story of a girl who believes her misfortune is reality. To this, I will say that reality and what we perceive as reality, is inconsequential to what makes up a life. Nothing is real, until it is personal.

I do not pretend to know what the meaning of life is, but I do know that it is a strange existence for those people who live on the fringe of our social fabric. This is the story of such a person. At its base, it is a tale of survival; at its best it is an amusing story of tenacity. If I could, I would leave the story untold. But I cannot. It will not leave my head, and so I write, in an attempt to remove the disillusionment of Americana, once and for all, from my mind.

Where shall I start this narrative? There are so many points of entrance. I would like to begin in recovery, but I cannot. First I must expose that which Lena seeks recovery from, or the mending procedure would be irrelevant.

Society works together to create the institutions that make our culture work in harmony. The main fabric of our society is created by interwoven standards of conduct. Our experience in social intercourse reinforces these standards of conduct. Religious institutions, education, structured work environments, all work in harmony to support and advance it. Like a coalition of troops that pledges its allegiance and loyalty, supporting the system that supports them. We are a team in America.

The consequence of non-participation in the American way of life can be painful, even deadly. Social out casting, imprisonment, poverty, irrecoverable salvation and death, all bear witness to the consequences of departing from the standards of conduct.

This fabric of society relies on its individual threads to give it strength. One thread, loosened and pulled, can produce an unraveling that ultimately creates an area of fringe.

With each new generation, the fabric grows in size and strength, color and texture. So does the fringe. Fringe people do not have the bond of loyalty to the greater good that the rest of our culture seems to adhere to. Participation in society is difficult, if not impossible, for people in the fringe.

Let me explain fringe people. You have met them. They are made from the same fabric as the rest of us. They look, talk, dress and, for most notations, are the same as the rest of society. But they are different. After you properly know them, you realize they are only partially attached to the fabric of society. Where most people are firmly established in the reality of that organization we call American, fringe people are merely dangling. They seem uncommitted and somewhat aloof from the whole membership idea. They ask the wrong questions and make their own rules. They have compulsive lives that frequently change. Fringe people are only attached to our culture by a small section in their life.

Knowing a fringe person, for most individuals, serves as a reminder of why we subscribe to the foundational principles of our culture: follow the rhythmic hymn of the commercial, work for the capital machine as if it were a grand adventure, and endorse this social arrangement as the ordnance of our God. These are the three stages of social and cultural programming: Subscribe, participate and then promote. This is the antithesis of the fringe.

There are three roads to the fringe. They all have one thing in common: Fear. The first is a purposeful removal of oneself from all the trappings of society. This is usually motivated by a social condition that creates fear of community and country.

Examples: Vietnam. Wal-Mart. OPEC. Computers. It doesn't really matter the cause. If an individual wishes to fear some thing, they will find a reason to fear it. Fear creates aversion. Aversion fosters hatred, which is why you must remove that thing which you fear. Or remove yourself. Welcome to the fringe.

This first group in the fringe usually produce fruit; children born to parents who despise the social institutions of society. Parents who fear social changes because those changes have an energy that cannot be controlled. Social change, while subject to manipulation by power and greed, is an uncontrollable force imposing itself on those who are more comfortable with the dependable nature of tradition.

Being born in the fringe can make for a difficult life. There is always the feeling that you're out of step with the rest of the troop. Always one note off in the band. We have social institutions that attempt in vain to connect the fringe student with the rest of the class. They educate and prepare the student to embrace the concept of unity and productivity. For children raised in the fringe, this looks like a suspicious attempt at indoctrination. The same is true in organized religion. Youth in the fringe may listen to the preacher pronounce the good people from evildoers, but they don't make a connection to themselves. It is as if the preacher is talking about someone else, somewhere else.

Because of the many comforts of our culture, a person must have an abundance of fear to take this first road to the fringe. It can be isolating and doesn't usually last a persons lifetime because of the hardships they must endure. Lena was born into this fringe condition.

The second road leading to the fringe is not as self-determined as the first. It is a psychosocial condition created through emotionally or physiologically damaging events. A person does not choose to have the experience, but once it has happened, an unconscious device is made available for protection against future events. The unconscious weapon creates a kind of mania, suspicion and disconnection from the rest of society. There again, welcome to the fringe.

A person with this condition may have the job, the house, and the family, but they do not place the same intrinsic value on the properties and positions of this American life. They consider the activities that mutate around them as merely a play on a stage. The normal rules of society have minimal meaning in this fringe. Every day on the news are reports of activities from fringe people: reckless politicians who get caught with their indiscretions, chief executive officers who cash in before the crash, husbands and wives who live separate lives of equal injustices, the hacker who spreads a virus. They do it because they can, not because it is right or wrong. For a person in the fringe right and wrong is not the underlying consideration for their action, lust and opportunity are. When Lena left her fringe family, she ended up here.

The third road to the fringe is well traveled. All you have to do is pick up the phone, tour the Internet, or walk into a particular building. It is the fringe institution. The members connect by sharing the same rebellion and fear toward a particular subject. While that may sound like most social groups, there is an important and specific criterion that puts a church or group in the fringe. It is a belief in something that contradicts socially accepted judgment. For example, believing that God can produce spontaneous healing in a believer is part of many religious beliefs. Not taking your child to the doctor when they are ill, even to the point of death, is the ideology of a fringe religious group.

The fringe institution is pregnant with possibilities that it never delivers: Aliens live among us, Nostradamas foretold the future, Satan and a vast right wing conspiracy controls the White

House. Many people find refuge form their fear or confusion of our society, in fringe groups. Lena did, but it was a short visit.

The problem with the fringe is that once a cut from the main fabric has been made, it is permanent. A person can work a lifetime to repair and reconnect to society, but there will always be evidence of the damage. A scar. You see, the fringe gives the main fabric of society something to report on, study, scorn, and ultimately condemn to the waste basket of life. This is what Lena doesn't want, but which seems unavoidable.

But why is there a fringe at all when social harmony and profitable value is the promise of participation? Why do some Americans loosen themselves from the fabric, and knowingly suspend in the fringe? At best, it's by accident, or a fear guided philosophy that leads people to develop lives that separate themselves from the culture. At worst, they have lost their mind and are incapable of relating to society. Some fringe people masquerade as being part of the main fabric, but it is always a poor fit. Life as a lie can be very uncomfortable.

Lastly, there are the remnants. This is not a path to the fringe existence, but rather a group of unfortunate individuals completely disconnected from the fabric of society. For many on the fringe, this is either their nightmare or their dream come true. Most fringe people exist either to understand and keep their connection with society, or to sever it entirely. For remnants, severing all ties to society has its benefits. You need not subscribe to changing social conditions; you can believe people fear you, or that you are extraordinarily wise and powerful. But remnants of our culture live in self-created delusions that are inconceivable to the rest of society: the cult that commits mass suicide, the mother who drives her children into a watery grave, the loner who buries his sexual prey in the woods behind the neighbor's house.

Remnants are not easy to spot, but eventually do get trapped. Society works to route out these individuals with watch lists, background investigations, fraud alerts, DNA tests. It is no great wonder that Remnants from the fringe have no status in the American dream. They have no obligation or investment in the American culture beyond their own self interest. They are the truly disconnected.

So is it good or bad, to be in the fringe? You might think you know the answer, but...*nothing* is *real*, not even the fringe, until it is personal.

One

I see the moon, and the moon sees me

As is usually the case, recovery is the simultaneous point of birth and death, a remaking of the person whom one can no longer suffer to live with. This is Ellen.

It is a very odd thing that most people who live in the fringe of our social fabric are not aware of how separated they have become from the rest of the culture, and of what a gift this could be. In order to survive, they live in denial. For those that are aware, the knowledge tends to be an additional tormenter. Most of the people in Ellen's life are aware of her instability, and try frantically to attach her to the main fabric of the community. However, on her 32nd birthday, Ellen became one of those individuals who decided to stop this mending process, release her grasp on reality, and live in the fringe. She was going to be whatever, and whomever, she really was. The problem was, the insanity that brought her to the edge of the cliff was very powerful, and letting go could be very dangerous.

The cliff, if you have never been there, is violent. It is the crevice that separates Deschutes County and Jefferson County in the center of the great State of Oregon. A dizzy look down will cancel any notion of play near or around the area. A small two-lane bridge allows travel from one side of the cavern to the other, and a state park sits on the south entrance to the bridge. They have since constructed a new bridge, but on the day Ellen visited, it was the old narrow one that she walked.

The state park has a three-foot rock wall bordering the cliff. The squirrels and lizards play on the Warning and Danger signs. At the bottom of the canyon the Crooked River winds through Central Oregon. A popular resort and golf course perches on the edge of the cliffs a few miles south. The cliffs are a point of fascination; unless you want to die. Then they become your enemy. For Ellen, the fear was not hitting the bottom; it was hitting a jagged side of a cliff before hitting the bottom. It was the full flight she wanted, and therefore had to take her dive from the bridge.

She parked the car at the small state park right before the bridge. She had always despised the car. Not that she wasn't grateful for the transportation. In reality, it was the first vehicle that was truly titled in her name. She hated it because it was a station wagon. The very icon of the nuclear family. Convention. It symbolized the squeeze that society put on her life in order to fit her into its mold. The car, like her, had been damaged. She purchased it off a wrecking lot for a few hundred dollars, borrowed from her mother-in-law. What was important was that she left town, she told herself, not what she left in.

But that was three years earlier. The moment at hand didn't require her to be angry. It was two o'clock in the afternoon, on a hot July day. The park had two circle drives. The first was for those wanting to park and use the restroom or picnic tables. The second circle farther north went to the rim of the gorge, where the rock wall separated the sight seekers from the walking path and the sheer cliffs. The signs on the wall read; 'Danger. Watch Children Carefully. Keep Pets On Leash.' There were no parking spaces there. It was a circle drive meant to give a person a view and turn around. Ellen parked in the road. She checked to see if traffic could get around her car. It could.

The park was nearly empty. A few visitors strolled about, (tourists she guessed) no children. That was good. It was a very warm day. The wind felt hot and dusty. The sky was a bright white. She had left her sunglasses in her purse in the car. She squinted in the direction of the bridge. The smell of the juniper trees caught her attention. The smell of gin. It had been a long time since she had gin.

She began to walk along the path that led to the bridge. It had been a long road here, she thought. She had practiced for this day all her life. Now her time was up. Today there would be no rescue. No God. No savior. No prince. Only freedom.

The exit from the walkway and the entrance onto the bridge and roadway was marked by a small set of stairs. "One step. Two step. Three step. Up. Now turn left," her head said. "Keep walking. No, don't think about the trucks passing. They won't hit you. Don't slow down. Don't lose your nerve. Just think. Freedom for a few seconds. You will be a bird. The only thing controlling your destiny will be physics. Gravity. You won't feel a thing."

She reached the center of the bridge where the arch on the understructure was at its highest point. The concrete railing she had been walking along is waist high. She stopped and put one leg over. She grasped the rail as a truck passing by almost blew her over. From the opposite direction, a truck honked deafeningly. "Fuck you!" her head screamed back.

Ellen looked down for the first time. The river far below was the color of coffee when it doesn't have enough creamer in it. She smiled. The air was soft and warm. Ellen tried to relax. The other leg went over. Anticipation began to take over. Her heart began to race with nervous excitement. Her head began to swim.

"Heeeeeyyy!!" The wind delivered a distant call, like a large bird announcing its territory.

"No!" Ellen panicked. "This is not happening. I can't share this. This is my moment." Even before she turned her head she felt someone approaching. Things began to move fast. Her leg had joined the other on the edge side of the bridge. Her bottom rested on the wide concrete wall.

"Wait!"

Squinting, Ellen saw a woman approach. She was small with long dark hair that moved wildly in the wind. Like Ellen, she was wearing shorts, t-shirt, and sandals. "Middle-class with a side of happiness," was Ellen's first thought. "Who the hell is this and how do I make her get lost," is her second. A truck blew by like an 80 mph gust of wind. It felt as if it passed only inches from her. "Time is running out on you, Ellen," a voice in her head whispered.

The woman was only a few feet away now. She had slowed her pace to almost stopping. She stretched out her hand. "What is she going to do," thought Ellen. "Save me? Grab me? Does she think I want to be saved?"

"What do you want?" Ellen hears herself ask. "Nothing is wrong, I just want to sit here."

"I just want you to wait a minute. Think about this." Her eyes were sincere and calm. Her outstretched hand was manicured. No ring there. She was slim, with a full mouth and large brown eyes. Her hair was dark with long strands of clear white mixed in. Fishing line, Ellen thought.

The woman continued to speak. "Don't give me a story. You wouldn't be here if nothing were wrong."

"Is something wrong, when I am making something right?" Ellen asked herself. "Irreparable damage. Is it something she had created, was born with, or born into? What is wrong Ellen?" She asked herself for the millionth time. "You are finished," was the answer that came back. "Nothing you have tried to accomplish has come to be. Your life is better off without you. Do this for Lena." She turned back to the open space waiting for her flight and took a breath. Her bottom inching toward the edge. "Now!" Her head shouted.

"Wait." The woman continued her interruption. "Not today. Just give it one more chance. You can do this tomorrow. Just for today... live. You can't change what has happened up to now, but you can live one last day, just as you would like it to be. Did you do that yesterday? No, you were thinking about today. Are you really prepared to let go of everything? Isn't there something left to do?"

"What? What are you talking about? There isn't anything I can do. Oh my god, you idiot. You don't know me. You don't have that *privilege*. I am not here to provide *you* with a savior situation. No offense lady, but go, get lost, I am not a piece of trash for you to salvage. I promise when this is over I won't tell anyone you were here."

The lady looked at her with a shared sadness. "Where does a person get a friend like that?" Ellen thought to herself. With regret Ellen swung her legs back to the roadside of the bridge and hopped down. "No peace here," she thought. "No peace anywhere," was the reply in her head. Walking past the lady she didn't even look at her. Who cares? This was becoming too much effort. All the talking and explaining just wasn't worth it.

"Courage, that is what you need Ellen," explained a voice in her head, or the stranger on the bridge. She was not sure which.

"You're right," replied Ellen. Turning on her heals; she walked past the lady with the dark eyes and secret smile, back to her spot on the middle of the bridge. Courage. She lifted herself up this time, and with both feet on the wall, she stood. The lady was talking but Ellen couldn't hear her anymore. She stretched out her arms. All she heard was the wind. She leaned forward and embraced the air. It greeted her into its world.

It is customary for a person's life to be reviewed in moments such as this, and Ellen's long decent to the bottom of the canyon was no exception. However, it was not her life she reviewed, but Lena's, as the river at the bottom of the canyon slowly grew closer.

Two

Mary, Mary, quite contrary. How does your garden grow?

In the early hours of morning, in the young part of 1966, two women sat politely at the dining table, looking at each other. The world was quiet. This was the first awkward moment of an undeniably painful twenty-year relationship, in which both women will refer back on this very conversation for both steadfastness and courage. Had either believed in regret, it would be that the conversation did nothing to change the direction, or persuade the young woman to quietly take her two small boys and go back home to her mother.

The men and the children in the house slept.

Marie lit a cigarette and sipped her coffee. She examined the woman sitting across the table from her. It was obvious Elizabeth needed a daddy for her two boys, and thought she had found just the right person in Marie's eighteen-year-old son. But Jimmy was five years Elizabeth's junior, and knew nothing about being a father; he lived the life of a boy.

Marie could also see what Elizabeth meant to Jimmy. She was beautiful in the 'new woman' kind of way. The modern woman she had seen in the magazines at the drug store. Elizabeth had a kitten kind of beauty. Soft golden curls, green eyes and high cheekbones. Her girlish figure hadn't changed after having two babies. She held a casual charm and a childlike nature.

"Elizabeth, you haven't a twig of understanding. Jimmy is just a child himself. Of all the men to get involved with, he is the worst kind. I love him because he is my son, but if he is anything like his father, your life will be hell." With this comment she smiled to herself, acknowledging the irony. She was having the conversation she wished someone had had with her before she married big Jim. It was as if Elizabeth hadn't even heard her.

Elizabeth defended herself. "I love him, and he loves me. Why can't you see this? You're his mother; you will always see him as a boy. To me he is the greatest man I've ever met." She paused, trying to come up with the words that would make everything better. But she couldn't.

"I love him and I know he loves me. We will make it work. Please Marie, give us your blessing. Above all else, Jimmy loves his family. We need you on our side...we are going to have a baby." She lowers her eyes. "We're going to have a baby."

Marie put her cigarette to her lips and slowly drew in the smoke. Marie was a practical woman. Nineteen years as a logger's wife had changed her from artist and teacher to homemaker and chief cook. She saw her dreams exit at the certainty of her permanent condition. She tended to the needs of a man and family. Exhausted, she hadn't the time to mourn for her loss. That would be an inefficient use of energy.

They sat in silence. When she spoke, it was with resolve. "You are in for hard times. Jimmy lives as a child in a man's world. He thinks only about playing hard and rough. He has been spoiled by his father and given the freedom to do as he pleases." She paused. "He expects that to continue forever. I think you should know he is as wild as boys come. I am to blame. I let his father raise him because it was easier than not. I *know* he is not prepared for family life, just as you know he is. But you only see what you want to see. You want to *believe* him into being what you need."

Angry, Elizabeth got up from the table. It was no use talking to Marie. She was like so many women of the previous generation, disillusioned and bitter. Still living in the 1940's. It was 1967, and the family had changed. Women and men had more equality, with closer relationships based on honesty. Relationships that evolve, without the expectations of a rigid social structure.

And so it was that Marie and Big Jim took care of the two little boys while Jimmy and Elizabeth went to Reno to tie the knot.

Three

Jack be nimble, Jack be quick, Jack jumped over the candlestick.

A dirty rutted road off the main highway leads to the base of a hill. The road makes an attempt to go up the hill, but loses its way near the top in numerous unsuccessful attempts to climb the steep rocky ledge. The dirt had been scraped away by trucks, leaving only jagged rocks to drive over in order to crest the hill. Once on top, the driving becomes a rutty one-lane path across a brushy plateau. Rocky outcroppings and clusters of trees give the ride a naturally beautiful face. There is no evidence of a human being except for the narrow path you are driving on.

After two miles you come to a barbed wire fence. TRESPASSERS WILL BE SHOT is the sign that greets you. You can continue to follow the road through the open barbed wire gate. Suddenly you are at a large clearing. A small cabin sits quietly in view. To your left is a collection of unspecified automobiles and appliances. As you continue toward the cabin you pass a chicken coop and outhouse.

This is the home Jimmy and Elizabeth built in 1967. Jimmy and Elizabeth planned to raise a family without the corrupt social contribution of the hippy generation. Although Jimmy wouldn't readily admit it, the idea was in reaction to the Vietnam conflict that was consuming the young men of the nation. With fear of the draft knocking on the front door, and the naivety of teenage lovers, Jimmy and Elizabeth worked out a plan to hide and live in the sagebrush and juniper trees of Rural Oregon.

With the help of Jimmy's parent's, they purchased 40 acres atop a plateau in central Oregon's high desert. It was accepted from the beginning that electricity, sewer and water were not going to be available for years, if ever. That is the consequence of living in the hills beyond the reaches of society.

They built the cabin over a summer, using the timber on the property. Like most grand building adventures, the end of the summer didn't mean the cabin was finished, just livable. Maybe someday they would put in windows. For now, plastic sheeting would have to do. The floor was plywood and the walls were covered with tarpaper. One long counter with a shelf under it ran the length of the inside. A picnic-style table in the center of the room had bench seating, enough for 12, with 6 on each side. A wood cook stove was in one corner, and a water tank was shelved near the ceiling. Underneath the water tank laid the remains of a barrel cut in half, with the edges turned in. A whole cut in the floor allowed the tank to drain under the house when the cap was removed.

The cabin was dim due to the lack of windows and artificial lighting. Kerosene lanterns were needed even in the daytime if a person were to see any detail at all. At the far end of the cabin was a ladder that ran up through the ceiling and into the second story floor. The second floor would eventually have six army cots, three on each side. Clothes boxes and blankets piled by each cot. At the far end of the room was a door leading out to the balcony. There the bed of the king and queen was found. It had a canopy and plastic sheeting that kept it from the elements. A white five-gallon bucket that said Army Surplus Peanut Butter was next to the wall. It served as the nighttime bathroom.

Once the cabin was built, they could begin to live their dreams. Jimmy would work as a logger when the offer was right, they would raise chickens and goats for the eggs and milk, and they would hunt deer and birds. They could live on practically no money. The plan was to have six children and teach them a new way of living. The children could make a difference in the world because they would have the values that come from growing up in a natural environment and from hard work, to the exclusion of the materialistic society.

It's easy to find something beautiful in their lives. The changing of the seasons brings changes to their family. Each New Year brought the birth of a new child. When they built the cabin, there were two small boys: a 4 year old red head named Web, and a 2 year old, curly black haired boy named Lee. Elizabeth was pregnant the year they built the cabin, and in mid July gave birth to their first girl, Punk. Punk had the Native American features Jimmy and Elizabeth wanted their country life to emulate. It was a sign from God.

Elizabeth kept busy with the kind of duties a frontier woman endured a century before. Hand washing laundry, milking goats, and making biscuits. Jimmy banged away at the house, and in the evening told stories to his new family of boys around an outdoor fire pit.

The seasons are harsh in this part of Oregon. The summer is hot and dry, desert like. Because of the high altitude, the winter is cold, snowy and very long. The first year they rested and enjoyed the fruits of their labor. Elizabeth had the new baby girl, and the two boys had their new father. He was the only father they knew. They cut a juniper tree for Christmas, and used the hood of a car to make a sled. The house filled up with Jimmy's parents and sisters and brothers during the holiday. It was a real celebration. That year was everything Elizabeth had imagined.

The second year at the cabin a two-seater outhouse was built farther away from the front door, and they were expecting another child. They had run out of water early in the summer, a constant worry for Elizabeth. She tried to hide it, but the new pregnancy made her moody. At least the boys were getting big enough to help out. Punk was one; old enough to let Web and Lee play with her.

In the fall Jean was born. She had blonde curly hair and a quiet sunny way about her.

Her family was everything to Elizabeth. Her life was similar to the pioneering days when the gender roles were well defined. Women knew their place, and men knew how to be in charge. Jimmy worked out of the area a lot that year, saving money to purchase a cow and two pigs, two horses. Web and Lee helped their dad build a pigpen, and the calf roamed free, as did the goats and horses. Elizabeth was always chasing them away from the clothesline in the summer.

Wild game was plentiful on their property, but refrigeration was not, so they had to eat the game fresh. Because of this, there was always the threat of the game warden coming on to the property and arresting Jimmy for poaching. It was a philosophical issue really, Jimmy believed he owned the game on his property, and he had the right to eat them if he so chose. That was the year they put up the TRESPASSERS WILL BE SHOT sign on the gate to their property. Jimmy felt he had every right to do whatever he chose to do on his property, and he announced this frequently at the local bar. He wanted to create fear in the federal game warden, but his boasting had just the opposite effect. It made him both a target and a challenge for the officers. Many nights the children could hear shouting and shots fired from the balcony. Jimmy, drunk and paranoid, was practicing for a battle with the government. His preparation did not pay off. When the government officers did come, it was when he wasn't there.

It wasn't long before four years had passed. The household had changed considerably. A fifth child was added. Harlan was a blonde quiet baby. Elizabeth joked with her mother-in-law that he was a mute. The two older boys went off to third and fourth grades. They walked to the bus stop at the bottom of the hill. It was 2.3 miles each way, and a point of pride for Jimmy, that his boys were growing up so strong, tough.

For Web and Lee, the best days were spent with the horses. Buckeye was a pony with a nasty habit of biting, but was short enough to jump on. Shorty was an old mare that wandered around slowly without paying much attention to anything. If she passed by you while you were on a rock pile or fence, you could climb onto her. Fun for the boys meant climbing trees and jumping onto Shorty. There was no saddle or reins, so they went wherever the horse wanted to go.

The cabin enjoyed entertainment that year. A radio hooked to a car battery sat on a shelf. An old bench car seat, out of the wrecking lot, worked as the gathering place for the family. In the evenings they would all pile on the seat and listen to Mystery Theater on the AM station. During the day Elizabeth enjoyed country music. She had perfected baking biscuits and pork rinds in the wood stove, and Jimmy had learned to make wine from currant berries, a dry bitter berry plentiful on the property.

Jimmy enjoyed his two older sons. They had been at the cabin four years. Web was 8, and Lee was 6. School was a struggle for the boys because of the long distance to the bus stop. During the winter they missed a lot of school. That didn't bother their parents. The way they saw it, their kids learned more at home than they did at school. Jimmy spent his time with the boys teaching them to hunt on horseback. He had a cap and ball pistol for which he made his own ammunition. It required him to keep black powder, lead and fuse wire.

In today's day and age, it would not be acceptable to have children caring for the needs of their siblings, but in the early 70's, when big families were still considered natural, Elizabeth didn't think twice about Punk and Jean being cared for by Web and Lee. She had six children by their sixth year at the cabin, and the two youngest were still in diapers. Cloth diapers. Web and Lee were 10 and 8, Punk was 6, Jean was 5, Harlan was 3 and the baby, Tony, was 1. It was the kind of celebrated large family one might imagine on The Walton's. But the Moran's were not the Walton's, and Silver Lake was not the Mountain.

By the sixth year, Web and Lee were big enough to watch over and care for Punk and Jean. To Elizabeth, the children seemed inseparable. Web, always the leader, filled the summer days with constant games. In the winter, he oversaw the walking to and from the bus stop.

Web and Lee had been attending the Silver Lake School for five years when Punk finally joined them in their walk to the bus stop. Elizabeth had waited until Punk was 6 because she was so small. Elizabeth worried she wouldn't be able to make the walk in the wintertime. But she need not have worried. Punk grew tough. She made friends, and every day the little girl with long braids and large dark brown eyes, went to school with her lunch of homemade pork rinds and biscuit's, looking like a little Indian girl. But even in the rural town of Silver Lake, the Moran children were considered odd.

Web and Lee were indifferent to school rules, playing rough and mean. Punk conversed with an unseen friend. They were never allowed to go to a friend's house, and no children from school visited the cabin.

Web and Lee walked fast down the hill on the way to school, sometimes running. If they missed the bus they would have to work all day at the cabin. On the way home though, the walk was uphill, and required a lot of effort. Punk was always tired and thirsty, especially in the fall when it was still very hot. On the walk home, they took the path along the cliffs instead of the road. It was a shorter way, but very rocky. It had all the makings of an adventure. There were bushes of currant, gray lizards that scurried across the path, steep jagged rocks that rimmed a deep and dangerous cliff. Punk loved to walk right on the edge. She loved it so much, that she asked to go that way again the next day. Web looked at her. He grinned an evil grin and put his face close to hers. His green eyes shone with malice.

Grinning and staring, he shoved her backwards, and she fell to the ground. She waited until he started walking off, and then she got up and followed. Punk knew better than to speak to him.

If Jimmy was at the cabin, Elizabeth was happy. She adored Jimmy. He had so much passion and commitment to their life. When times were difficult, he always found a way out. One year they bought a glasscutter and made glasses out of coke bottles and gave them as Christmas gifts. Elizabeth tried to make the holidays special even though they lived so far away from others in the community. Halloween was a time to make pies, and Christmas was a time for knitting.

Always, when Jimmy was around, it was a time to drink and raise ruckus. The family wasn't the only inhabitants on the property. After the first couple of years, Jimmy started bringing friends from the logging camps home to hunt on the property. During these times, there was always a big party at the edge of the cliffs behind the house. A rocky path wound its way to an area that has a fire pit and picnic table. Stumps and large rocks ring the fire pit for additional seating. On the ledge of the cliff the desolate valley stretched below. Sagebrush and juniper trees extend out as far as you can see without a road or house on the horizon.

There were always long weekend parties during the summer. Jimmy would bring his logging buddies, and sometimes their families, back to the cabin. Everyone would sit around the fire at the back cliffs and watch the sunset, telling stories and drinking. In the morning, when everyone was still sleeping in the cabin, Punk and Web would sort through the remnants of the party.

The fire pit held embers that could be coaxed back to life with trash. Sometimes beer bottles still contained their liquid. One such morning Punk found an unopened bottle and tried to open it. She wrapped her little hands around the neck and turned on the cap. It didn't even budge. She tried prying the metal cap with her teeth. That didn't work. She sat on a stump and thought a moment. Harlan had joined her and was poking at the fire pit with a stick, looking for embers. He was talking to himself about fires being hot.

Punk set the bottle down next to a tree. She went back to the porch of the cabin and picked up the pocketknife that lay on top of the chopping block. Back to the tree she ran. Kneeling by the bottle, she opened the knife. Timidly she stabbed at the bottle cap. Her aim was good, but the tip of the knife didn't pierce the cap as she had expected. Again she tried, but the tip wouldn't go through. Finally, she wrapped her hand around the neck of the bottle, and raised the pocketknife high. She knew that if she hit the cap hard enough, it would pierce through the metal. She squeezed the knife hard and plunged it through the air.

Missing the cap, she plunging the knife into the flesh between her thumb and index finger. Shocked, she stared wild-eyed at the knife sticking out of her hand. She screamed and ran.

Back in the cabin, Elizabeth was cooking eggs in a cast iron skillet over the wood stove. She looked up when she heard the scream. Running toward her was Punk: shrieking at the top of her lungs, eyes bulging, and a knife sticking out of her hand. She quickly removed the knife and consoled Punk to stop making such an awful noise. She pinched the wound hard, and wrapped her hand with cheesecloth. The guests and other children ran over to see, but it was too late. The wound was covered, and Elizabeth told her to hush. She shouldn't be playing with knives. Wiping her face, Punk went outside. She hadn't forgotten about the unopened bottle. She would hide it until she could find something to open it with.

Creative ways to keep her sanity became necessary for Elizabeth after the sixth child had arrived. Six to feed, six to clothe. Without electric power, or running water there was no such thing as clean. Living in the hills meant no library, no television, no church, and no friends. Six children meant there was no such thing as free time. It had to be good enough that the children were fed, and had a warm place to sleep. Elizabeth learned not to look to closely at the details in her life.

Elizabeth got by most of the time on hand me downs, and donations from her in-laws, but the rugged lifestyle was taking its toll on everything. The roof leaked, the floor of particleboard was eroding, the plastic on the windows was shredded. Jimmy had a temporary solution. They would earn the money to buy the repairs by salvaging copper. The price of copper was going up. It was his plan to collect old wiring and strip it for the copper. He thought it was a good plan because Web was 12, Lee was 10 and Punk was 6. They could do some of the work. There was also some brush piling at a logging camp he could take the kids to do. After all, it was part of his overall plan to have a family that worked together.

1974 was a long summer. Elizabeth stayed at the cabin with the three youngest, Jean 5, Harlan 4, and Tony 3. Jimmy took Web, Lee and Punk with him to the logging camp, 98 miles south. At the camps, Punk did everything she could to keep up, but the boys did better than her. Even then, the plan only lasted three days. Jimmy did not take into account that he would have to care for his children. He had brought them to teach them how to work, and they complied as best as they could. He didn't realize they would have the same kind of needs other children have.

At the campfire that night, loggers sat on stumps of wood and talked about the days cut. Old Paul Miller, the resident camp host, commented about the kids.

"Those kids of yours didn't do half bad today. I know some green horns that don't work that hard. What's your secret?"

"Yeah," said Jimmy. "They're ok. A bit complaining at times, though. Missing their pets. It's a regular zoo at the cabin." He paused and drank his beer. He looked at Old Paul and grinned. "I teach 'em to work, and if they don't, they get switched. That's the key. They have to know who's boss."

"My old lady does the spankin' at our house. It's always a big screamin' fight. I have to go outside to get away from the noise." Paul shook his head and looked down at the dirt.

"That's all wrong. You gotta not put up with no screaming or cryin'. You see, the trick is not the switchin, that's just part of it. First, ya make 'em go and find the stick you're goin' to use on them. Each one has to find their own switch. That keeps them anticipatin' it. They'll be cryin' about how sorry they are, and won't do it again. But ya can't let up, or they won't believe ya next time. Then, after they get the stick, ya have to bend it real good to make sure it ain't gonna break when you whip 'em."

Jimmy drank from his bottle of beer. The campfire had grown quiet. All eyes were on him in the dim firelight. He smiled into the fire. He felt altogether proud of his experience and skill at parenting.

Web, Lee and Punk lasted two more days. They worked hard piling brush left over from the timber sale. In the evening they began to complain about being thirsty, being tired and missing their pets. Around the campfire on the third night, a camper suggested that they return to their mother, as the children were needing attention. Angry, Jimmy looked at the children in the firelight. They were covered in dirty cuts and scratches, matted hair hung in their faces. They were quiet from exhaustion, eating oatmeal with hands and faces that were covered in pitch. He looked away.

Before the first light of the next morning, Jimmy loaded up the three children, still in their sleeping blankets, into the cab of the pickup truck, and started back to the cabin. When they were fully awake, he let them know what a disappointment they had been to him. He had thought better of them at the cabin, but they had proved him wrong. They were not as capable as he thought, and he was going to have to do a better job teaching the value of work. The children rode in silence. They knew better than to speak to their father unless he was asking a direct question. It was one of many times they would disappoint their father.

As the children grew up, they learned about the land they were born to. It was a rugged existence. The summer was spent gathering what was needed to make it through the long winters. There was wood to cut and stack, hay to purchase and store for the two horses, two goats and calf, a new batch of baby chicks to incubate from eggs, and monthly trips to the USDA surplus store in Klamath Falls. There you could get flour, honey, peanut butter and other staples, in five gallon buckets. Families were only allowed to receive once a month, so Elizabeth took every opportunity to stock up, whether or not they needed it. The surplus store also had wool blankets, cots, diapers, soaps, matches and other sundries, for little or no cost. Every year was the same; free was all she could afford. So whatever was free, she brought back as much as possible.

As the children grew older, so did the parents. Jimmy spent a great deal of time away from home, working. He would come back once or twice a month, with a new pet for the kids. They had a collection of many different animals by that time. They included three Canadian geese, two goats, and five dogs of various breeds. He liked the homecomings and told Elizabeth so. She tried to make the best of it. He would arrive home in the middle of the night or early hours of the morning, drunk and happy to see her. He would always have a large supply of cash, beer and vodka. Elizabeth would joke that it looked like he robbed a liquor store.

During the days Jimmy was home, Elizabeth would take the cash and go into Silver Lake, or farther on to Klamath Falls. Sometimes she would go to the bar, sometimes to a friend's house, and then pick the kids up after school. They loved to ride home with her because that meant no long hike after the bus dropped them off. For Punk, it also meant her brother wouldn't hurt her.

Summers at the cabin were the best time of year. The days were long, and the children could spend them exploring the acres of trees and rocks. Punk knew where every currant berry bush was, and when they were going to be ripe. She knew where to find the horses when no one else could. She could walk the entire fence line around their forty acres without getting lost, and she could climb up the outside of the balcony like it were a jungle gym.

They had added a smoke house the 10th year so they could cure meat and keep it longer. The 10th year also had a series of unfortunate accidents that kept Elizabeth in a constant state of crisis. In the fall, Harlan slipped off a cliff and broke his wrist. It didn't get set properly, and he had trouble using it. Lee got pneumonia and missed an entire year of school. Punk got hit in the head with a baseball bat. The school wasn't sure what happened. The blow cracked her skull above her right eye, giving her face a disfiguring sag. By February, Elizabeth was out of her mind with cabin fever. For the first time since they moved there, Elizabeth began to dream about a home with a phone.

It was 1978 and Elizabeth and Jimmy had been married eleven years. When February arrived and Jimmy hadn't been home for a month, Elizabeth knew he wasn't logging in the snow. The camps had been shut down since Thanksgiving. She had no way to reach him or anyone else. She felt trapped. When he finally arrived, she said she was finished with everything. She just couldn't take it anymore.

"You're being hysterical. Come on now. Kids get sick. They're tough."

Elizabeth was just getting started. "Where have you been? Do you ever think that we may be up here with no water or food? Stranded? What if one of the kids got seriously sick? Lee has pneumonia. Don't you even give a shit if he dies? What am I suppose to do? If it wasn't for the school nurse taking him in to the doctors in Klamath Falls, he could have died. He still is sick..."

"You did fine," Jimmy replied. "What could I have done Elizabeth? What more could I have done than what you already did? You act like if I had been here it wouldn't have happened or something. Kids get sick, and then they get better. It's nothing to get hysterical about."

"You act like all you have to do is come here once in awhile and act like a man- shooting your gun, hauling the water. Then you can just disappear again, and that being here for more then a week doesn't matter."

"What do you want from me? I give you whatever you want. I provide for this family the best way I can. I love the kids. I spend as much time with them as I can. Life isn't free Elizabeth. Someone has to work."

"So that's where you've been? Working? Where? Really Jimmy! What logging outfit is working right now in the snow? Where is the money? Two months Jimmy. You've been gone two months!"

"It hasn't been two months. I went down to the Sierra Nevada with Old Paul. He got a scoop on a motorcycle there. He needed a ride to pick it up. I couldn't say no. You know how many times he's bailed me out?"

"If you were here more, you wouldn't need to be bailed out. I don't want to do this anymore Jimmy. I don't want to be here without you." Elizabeth called upon her Irish stubbornness. "I need money to go to my mom's in Sunny Valley. I'm sick of living off beans and eggs, freezing my ass off trying to keep a stove burning, and keeping the goats and chickens fed. I've had plenty of time to think about this. Whatever you think you are doing, it's not enough."

A momentary silence. Jimmy considered the prospect of trying to talk her out of her anger. Then changed his mind. He was angry with her for wanting to destroy his life.

"You want food; I'll get you venison. We'll have a nice dinner. Why don't you make some tea and biscuits? You'll see. Hey..."

Elizabeth got up and walked across the room to the car seat leaning against the wall. Laying down, she gritted her teeth, covered up with a wool blanket and closed her eyes. Jimmy stood there a moment, and then climbed the ladder up to the kid's room.

Punk lay on her cot, still dressed. Her arms were wrapped around the clown she got at the nurses office at school. He sat on the end of the cot. Web and Lee rose from their beds and went over to their father, who did not notice how close they were to becoming young men.

Ignoring the boys' attention, Jimmy said, "Hey Punky, want to go hunting?"

"Hey, yeah!" the boys responded enthusiastically.

Jimmy stood up. "Go back to bed. I am not taking you anywhere. Your mom told me she has had to do all the fires. She had to feed the animals. I taught you to hunt because I thought you wanted to be men. You don't deserve to hunt if you can't do the man's work when I am gone. I am going to take Punk, and you are going to do women's work for a while. Now get back to bed. We'll talk about this tomorrow." He pinched his oldest daughter on the arm, and she got up too follow him down the ladder.

The man and the girl walked outside into a cold winter evening. The snowflakes drifted slowly down in the windless night. It was quiet. Jimmy tied a rope onto Shorty's halter and began to lead him toward the southern end of the property. Punk followed closely with her head down, watching the black leather boots in front of her. She was cold.

The leather boots stopped abruptly. She stopped. When they began to move again, she hastened after them. She gave no indication that she knew what they were doing or where they were going. Her fingers and nose were cold, but her eyes never left the boots in front of her. They were black against the white ground covering.

Again the boots stopped. Then stayed. A loud crack broke the cold silence. Punk cried out, fell to her knees, hands over her ears. The horse leapt to the side. Jimmy stood still, not sure if he got the kill, or if it ran off.

"Punk, hold the rope. Get up, and hold the rope for me. I don't want Shorty running off." Punk knew Shorty never ran anywhere under any circumstances, but she got to her feet and took the rope.

A few moments later her father returned to her. His voice was excited. "Come on. I got it." He was smoking a cigarette. His hands were covered in blood. They went to where the animal lay. The stomach had been cut open and the organs lay in a pile outside the body, filling the air with white steam. He had slit the animal's throat, but left its head attached. He reached inside its chest and pulled and cut, until he had its heart free.

"Here Punk, this is your job. You carry this. It's important. It's a present for mommy. Put out your hands. Put them together." He placed the heart in her hands. "Now don't drop it."

"Oh, it's warm," she said.

"Yes, that's right. It will keep your hands warm."

He picked up the carcass and placed it over Shorty, tying its legs together underneath. They started back the way they came. Punk watched the black boots in the white snow, trying to avoid looking at the warm mass of blood and tissue she carried with both hands.

They ate the deer that month, and then came the spring. There hadn't been any more talk about leaving the cabin. That summer Jimmy purchased a small Datson pickup for Elizabeth to use when he was gone.

It is with precision the way children know when their life has been changed forever, with a definite end to the known, and an entering into an incomprehensible new beginning. In a sudden moment of clarity, they find that yesterday is gone forever. To the adults, time and experiences melt together. Not so for the children. On the end of the eleventh season at the cabin on the plateau, Elizabeth and Jimmy begin to trip over the mess of dreams they fell short of attaining.

It had been a hot summer and Elizabeth wanted to get away from the never-ending work at the cabin. Jimmy had been away for three weeks, as she knew he would be. Logging was a summer job, and he was at a camp in the Blue Mountain Range. The thought of a cool mountain stream and other logging families enticed her to make plans to surprise Jimmy with a visit.

They traveled in the Dotson pickup. Web, Lee and Punk rode in the back, with boxes of canned food, bedding, and Snoopy, the family dog. In the cab, Elizabeth had the three small children, Jean, Harlan and Tony. Elizabeth left in the evening, so the children would be sleeping most of the drive. It was a nine-hour trip, which she made with only two stops. They arrived at the Sparta Logging Sale at 8:00 the next morning.

Elizabeth spotted the old Jeep Wagoner Jimmy's father had bought them, and pulled into the campground. As they drove by, other campers in the area turned to look at them curiously. As soon as they stopped, Web and Lee jumped out of the back and ran into their father's tent. It was a large green canvas tent, set up with poles and ropes. The corners were tied to trees and the roof pole was nearly 10 feet in height. The door was a large flap, tied shut.

Elizabeth entered the tent where Web and Lee had already disappeared. She paused a moment to let her eyes adjust to the dimness. She first saw the boys, standing by their father, who was lying in a sofa bed. They were excitedly telling him about making fishing poles to fish with. Jimmy was silent, as was the girl lying next to him. Elizabeth was speechless, and asked the boys to wait outside. They had to be told twice.

Jimmy, caught in the act of infidelity, did what he did best, pretended it wasn't happening.

"Hey Elizabeth! I wasn't expecting you. Uhhh...."

"How could you do this? You have six kids. I take care of six fucking kids in the middle of nowhere, living your fucking dream. So you can fuck around. You no good piece of shit. You tell me you are working so hard, that you live for this family. You rotten son of a bitch, I hope you burn in hell for the lies you have created. I live in those lies Jimmy. I live for you and the kids, and this is all I get from you? You can't live without fucking around? Our life is not enough for you? I have given up everything for this fantasy life you wanted, and this is what I get- a man who screws around, in front of the kids and me? Get this whore out of here!"

"Come on now Elizabeth, don't be like that. It's not Veronica's fault. She has nowhere to go. Let's just leave her out of this."

Veronica got up and began to put her jeans on. She wanted to leave the tent, but Elizabeth was blocking the only exit.

"Let Veronica go outside, so we can talk."

Veronica picked up her cigarettes and lighter, and went outside barefoot. Six faces greeted her, ranging in ages from three to fifteen. "Hi," Jean said. Web and Lee walked off to the creek, Tony and Harlan were playing in the dirt with sticks, and Punk just sat and stared at Veronica, while Jean chatted about the food they had brought to Daddy.

Four

There was an old woman who lived in a shoe, she had so many children, she didn't know what to do.

The tearing apart of a family is a raw scene. The pain is so great; the participants often take the quick approach, like removing a bandage or pulling a sliver. There is no such thing as a clean break, but Elizabeth did her best. She loaded the food and bedding from the truck into the Wagoner, and told the kids to get in. They traveled for two more days, to the opposite end of the state, reaching her mother's house in the evening.

Grandma lived in a singlewide mobile home, in a park. Her house was full of the grandma kinds of things you would expect. Ornamental figurines filled the shelves and counter tops. She took one look at the dirty-faced children her daughter had brought with her, and shook her head.

"The older boys will have to sleep in your truck; I don't have the room for them. And give them baths before they touch anything." Elizabeth silently obeyed. She would do whatever her mother asked. Her mother always asked a lot, and gave nothing in return. But that was the price Elizabeth had to pay. She bathed Harlan, Tony, Jean and Punk, and put them to sleep on the living room floor. Web and Lee she sent back out to the truck with the dog for the night.

What was a great loss of dignity for Elizabeth was a great event for the Moran kids. They loved everything about the little neighborhood. Most of all, they loved the lawns and sprinklers. A simple pleasure for other children was a combination of scientific miracle and pure clean fun. Nowhere had they experienced greener grass or more refreshing water.

Punk sat on the porch steps. It was already very warm. Grandma said she would turn on the sprinkler in a little while. She wasn't sure what a little while meant to grandma, but to her it had already come and gone. The sun was hot on the top of her head. She looked at the purple flowers. This sure was different from their cabin.

Lee was walking toward her from around the side of the trailer. "Hi Punk. Wanna see what I found?"

"What is it?"

"It's a little house. It's really old."

She looked at him suspiciously. "Why?"

"'Cause its fun. Come on."

She got up from the porch and followed him around the corner of the building. Just like he said, there was a small brown wooden building partially hidden by blackberry brush. Web stood near it, looking rather pleased with himself.

"Hey Punk, we found doll stuff in this house. Wanna see?" He opened the door slightly. Without hesitation, Punk reached out and opened the door. She had no intention of going inside the small windowless building. When she leaned forward to peer in, she felt a push from behind, and then the door slammed against her.

"Hey! Let me out. Let me out!" She began to pound on the door. It wouldn't budge. She stopped and tried to let her eyes adjust to the darkness. A slit of light near the ceiling was all that was visible.

In the darkness she felt movement in the air above her. Then she heard a low buzz near her right ear. In an instant, she knew what it was. A beehive was coming alive. Her words turned into a scream, and she pounded on the door with her fists. The wasps swarmed her head and arms, as she flailed and punched in the air.

Suddenly the door swung open, and she ran shrieking across the back yard. Running and screaming, the legion of angry wasps pursued her across the yard and through the front door. She ran as fast as she could through the narrow trailer house until she reached the bathroom at the far end. She yanked open the door and slammed it behind her. Still crying and breathing hard, she held onto the doorknob. She thought momentarily that she had outrun them, and was safe. Then she felt them in her shirt. "Ooooohhhh!!!"

The bathroom door swung open and Elizabeth began to slap her on the back, crushing the wasps between her shirt and her skin.

"Okay, okay, I got them. Let me see." She lifted her shirt up and began to brush the still writhing wasps from her skin and shirt. "It's okay now, it's okay. I got them. It's over."

Grandma was standing behind her mother shaking her head. "Oh, poor thing. Oh, you poor baby. Hasn't anyone taught you about wasps? You shouldn't play by their nests."

Punk looked at the two women who were cleaning her. She opened her mouth to speak, her large brown eyes shining wide with terror, but no words came out.

Later that evening, when the children were sleeping, Elizabeth's mother said enough was enough. The children were just too much for her to take. Elizabeth would need to find a more permanent place to live, and as soon as possible.

Elizabeth knew this, but it hurt to hear it. After all, it was a time of transition, and she needed a little help. But help wasn't forthcoming. She left the next day, and returned to the cabin. It was a short visit. Just long enough to give the animals their freedom, pack up the leftovers of a life that had been wrong from the start, and travel back down the dusty road one last time. The Jeep Wagoner was filled with the cries of six children, all wanting to know about the fate of the horses, of the chickens, of the goat. Six children crying and fighting with each other, all wanting to know where they were going to live, and what they were going to do.

Elizabeth stopped the Wagoner. In an angry voice she addressed the rough group of four boys and two girls. "I don't know what we are going to do, so don't ask me! I don't know what will happen to the cabin, or the animals, and I *don't care*. We are going to leave this place, and you will *not* talk about it *ever again*." With all the rage and fear in her she yelled a final instruction, "Now sit down and shut up, before I make you walk!"

With that, Elizabeth moved the kids from the Cabin in Silver Lake. Not only had her dreams of home and family been shattered, she had been left to clean up the mess. Well, she was not going to do that. That task was impossible, as she had six children reminding her *everyday* what a mess she had made of her life. No one looked back as they traveled down the dirt road and around the corner.

Five

If wishes were horses, beggars would ride.

Elizabeth relocated to a ranching community, eighty miles away. Gary, a rancher she had met during a night at the bar, had a rental house. He was willing to let her move into it without rent, until she could afford to pay. Until then, she could feed his horses and help him on his ranch.

Jimmy and Elizabeth's dream lasted eleven years. They blamed each other for its miserable end, but it was reality that ended their dream. Jimmy disappeared from his beloved state of Oregon, embracing the life of a dead-beat Dad, dodging child support by moving from state to state. Elizabeth got a job as a waitress at the only bar in town.

The children had been attending the school in the town of Pigeon for five weeks when Elizabeth was called in to meet with the principal. He sat at his desk, feeling important, but having done nothing yet that day. He had taken the job the previous year after being removed from his position in Portland. He was determined to do as little as possible, and enjoy as much as he could, in this cow town. He found it ironic that the cheap suits he wore impressed the residents of the community, commanding the respect that had always eluded him in the city.

She looked like an easy woman. Tight wrangler jeans, a satin western-style shirt partially unbuttoned, and cowboy boots. She was younger looking than he imagined a woman with six children to be. She had green eyes and curly brown hair. She had a thin face with high cheekbones. His new single life could make room for this woman, but the kids would be an issue he would not want to touch.

"May I call you Elizabeth?"

"Yeah," she said with a smile.

"It's nice to meet you. It's such a small school, that the addition of six children is quite a growth in attendance. How do you like the community so far?"

Elizabeth didn't care about any of his talk. She had other things to do than talk about the children. It had been her experience that meetings at school were never positive experiences, so she came emotionally prepared to defend herself. Mr. Dunn stood up and introduced himself, and reached out to shake her hand. She nodded at him and sat down. It did not escape her notice that he was checking her out. She knew she was a beautiful woman. She didn't need a weasel of a man to stroke her ego.

"It's fine. What did you want to talk to me about?"

"I wanted to ask about your children's previous school experience. It says on their enrollment that they went to Silver Lake K-12. Is that their entire education so far?"

"Yes. That's what I said on the paper, why would I..."

"Well... my conversations with their teachers is that they are not up to the grade levels they are enrolled in. I am thinking maybe a change in grade levels would be a good idea."

"No, I don't think so. I want the kids to finish school on time. I am not going to have them held back because your school measures them differently than another school." She took a deep breath and softened her voice. "You see, my kids lived way out of town, and didn't have good attendance because of bad weather. I have always left their education to the teachers, so if they are not at the level they are supposed to be at, it is the school's fault and you should do whatever it takes to fix it."

"I see. I agree that the school is responsible for teaching, but you see, their attendance records show they were absent more than they were at school. Kids don't learn very well that way." He paused. "To put it straight to you, Lee is in the ninth grade, but reads at the second grade level." He looked down at a sheet of paper. "Web reads at the fifth grade level. Lena is developmentally delayed in language and is behind in mathematics. Your two youngest children Jean and Harlan seem to be doing okay, and of course Tony is in the first grade, so he is right where he should be. Do you see where I am going with this?"

"No, I don't, and her name is Punk."

"Huh? Who is Punk?"

"Lena, she goes by Punk ever since she was a baby."

"Oh, I am sorry. I didn't know she had a nickname. I'll make a note of that." He paused. "Whether your older boys remain in their current grades or not, they will not graduate on schedule."

"Yes they will. They will graduate, or leave school when they are 18. What do you think would be better for them?"

"Well, of course they would be better off if they graduate, but I don't see how they can."

"Why don't you just let them do their best, and worry about this when the time comes? I think the football and basketball teams will give Web and Lee the interest in attending school that they have lacked. As far as Punk goes, she will catch up. If she can stay out of trouble." Elizabeth smiled to herself. Her oldest daughter was a bit of a free spirit.

"That's something else I wanted to talk to you about. Lena... uh....Punk's.. teacher believes she is chewing snuff and spitting on the carpet in the classroom."

"That's ridiculous… and gross."

"She also believes that …Punk…. brought a mason jar of gin to school and hid it in the girl's bathroom."

"You know, it sounds like this teacher is having some problems in her classroom. There is no possible way Punk could get those things. The only one who drinks and chews is her father, God knows where he is. Even if someone gave her Copenhagen or gin, I'm not sure what I am supposed to do about it. I mean, if students are doing this, it's the teacher who really needs to find a way to handle it."

Mr. Dunn cleared his throat and put his elbows on the desk. He laced his fingers together in a prayer position. This was not going as well as he had hoped. This mother seemed indifferent to his concerns.

"Why don't we do this? Let's get together and talk about this in a couple of months. You could be right about the sports for the boys. It could be exactly what is needed to get them to attend school. I will speak to Punk's teacher and see if maybe there could be another child involved with these problems. Would you like to speak with her teacher, Mrs. Irons, directly?"

"No," Elizabeth said, without an explanation or excuse. She got up from her chair, and put her purse strap over her shoulder.

"I have to go, I am helping out serving lunch at the Watering Hole. It was nice talking to you." She started toward the door.

"Yes, thank you for coming in. Oh, there is one more thing…"

Elizabeth turned around and waited.

"The school nurse was here last week. She said that all the Moran kids have lice. There are no other Moran's at this school, so I assume she was talking about your children. I asked her for treatment products, given that I know how difficult it is for you to get into a town with a pharmacy. She left enough for all the children. She said to just follow the directions and you shouldn't have any problems."

Elizabeth took the brown sack he held out to her without looking at him, and left the office. Life sure wasn't how she imagined it would be.

Six

Birds of a feather flock together, and so do pigs and swine.

Every passing year is as difficult as the previous. Elizabeth signed up for welfare and food stamps, and worked for tips at the Watering Hole. She couldn't afford the power, so the house was always dark. She had a load of wood delivered, so they had heat. They ate a lot of sandwiches and drank a lot of powdered milk. The children got free lunches at school, the only whole meal of the day. They never had hot water, because there was no power, but everyone was already used to heating water on the wood stove, and dumping it into the tub.

The way Elizabeth saw it, at least she still lived in the country, where she felt safe. She could collect welfare, food stamps, and work under the table was easy to find. The kids could go wherever they wanted, without getting into too much trouble. Web and Lee were the stars of both the basketball and football teams. They became overnight successes, winning games on the home court and away. Both boys were tall and mean, knocking anyone down who got in their way. Elizabeth had to laugh at the antics they pulled, in and out of the games. They were wild like their dad, and she couldn't do a thing about it, except be grateful the town was too small to have a police department.

They had been living in the house behind the bar for three years, when Gary asked her to marry him. It was a busy Friday night at the Watering Hole. It wasn't just a bar. It was a family experience. Divided into two parts, drunk ranchers on the bar side, and the football team on the kid's side. The small building drowned in noise.

Gary came in and put a dollar's worth of dimes in the juke-box. He had a plan. When their song began to play, he would ask her to slow dance. He would ask her to marry him on the dance floor. He was a bit nervous, but a drink would loosen him up. Elizabeth was an amazing woman, and her kids would finally fill his old house with life. Most of all, he wanted to help make her life better. She worked so hard, for so little. If she just had a good man to give her a home, she would be a damned good wife.

Gary joined his brother at one of the tables. It was crowded, and beer bottles tipped over when his chair bumped the table. Elizabeth joined them between waiting on the demanding customers. She wasn't technically an employee, because she worked for tips only. She managed to get to a table before they complained about their order. Then she would turn on the charm and humor. Everyone loved her. Well, all the guys anyway.

Gary had Elizabeth sitting on his lap when the song began to play. He paused for just a moment, considering once again if he really wanted to do this. Then he downed the rest of his beer and took her hand, leading her to the small space designated as the dance floor. She was in good humor, as always, laughing and playing with his beard. He took a deep look into her green eyes. The dim light made focusing difficult, and the volume of the crowd made it impossible to hear his own voice. He put his mouth to her ear, and said, "Elizabeth, will you marry me?"

Elizabeth pulled back sharply and stopped swaying to the music. She was gripping his arm and shaking her head yes. They embraced, and then left the bar to go back to his place.

Elizabeth got home at 2:00 that Saturday afternoon. Web and Lee were gone somewhere with friends, Punk and Jean were reading. Punk had fixed Harlan and Tony oatmeal over the woodstove, which had burnt. The house smelled like scorched food. Harlan and Tony were playing on the kitchen floor, still in their underwear and t-shirts. Dirty dishes were stacked on the counter.

"Punk……….. Punk! Get in here!"

Punk arrived in the kitchen, mute and sullen.

"What have you been doing? I asked you not to leave a mess like this again. Why aren't the boys dressed?"

"I was reading. I was going to do it later, 'cause I didn't know you were coming home so soon. Harlan and Tony don't have any clean pants, and we are out of soap. You didn't leave money for the store."

"Couldn't you have them put on some dirty clothes for to-day, until I get some soap?"

Punk just looked at her. She didn't see the difference between wearing dirty clothes or no clothes if they weren't going anywhere.

"Okay, take them into their room and pick out something for them to wear from the dirty pile. I think the cat peed on the pile in the hall, so don't get anything from there. Then brush your hair, and ask Jean to brush hers. We are going to Gary's house for dinner."

Gary's house was large compared to where they were living. It was located a mile or so out of town. It had a big tree in front, and a fence all the way around it. The best part about going to Gary's was that he had a television. Although it was 1981, television was still new to the Moran family. When they arrived for dinner, it was getting dark, and they all went inside to see what was on TV. The living room was sparsely furnished and had a polished wooden floor. Everyone took off their shoes on the porch, and ran across the floor in an attempt to slide.

The sofa became crowed with kids elbowing to get away from sitting to close too each other. Once the TV was turned on, they settled down to watch *Mutual of Omaha's Wild Kingdom.*

Elizabeth and Gary went into the kitchen to work on dinner and have a drink. They visited quietly about their future. Gary heard Missy, his cow dog and best friend, scratch at the back door, and he went to let her in.

In the fringe, one unpredictable event can create a significant change in the course a person's life will take. This was one of those events.

In the living room all was going well, until Missy came in the room seeking attention. Her head went from lap to lap, getting stroked. When she got to the end of the sofa, she laid her head on Punk. Looking down, Punk saw a long string of saliva trail across her pants.

"Yuck, get away from me." She shoved the dog's face off her lap, and then kicked it with her bare foot. Without warning, Gary bolted out of the kitchen and headed straight for her.

Gary picked Punk off the sofa by both her arms and shoved her away from the couch. "You little bitch. Don't you ever touch my dog!"

"Hey, it slimed me. Maybe you ought to teach it not to slime people and then it won't get kicked!"

Without hesitation, Gary raised his hand and delivered a slap across her left cheek. Shocked, Punk ran out the front door, slamming it as she went. In the darkness, she stuffed her feet into her shoes and walked out to the road. There she began to run, with tears rolling down her face. She ran the mile back into town, and into the dark house behind the bar.

Once in the house, she began to think. One thing she knew beyond a doubt, she wasn't doing *this* any more. This was not the mother, the father, the school, the anything that she wanted. She went to her room. Looking around she could find nothing she wanted to take with her. She went into her mother's room. Beside the bed was a nightstand. In the dark she pulled the drawer open. In it she found coins and letters. One letter was from Marie Moran. She opened it.

The letter described her disappointment in Elizabeth for not taking Jimmy back after their argument. She recounted her conversation 14 years earlier, when Elizabeth accepted all that came with being a logger's wife. In the letter she begged Elizabeth to call Jimmy and reconcile. She gave the number where he could be reached.

Punk tore that portion of the letter off and put it in her pocket. Suddenly, she felt better. She wiped her nose on her sleeve, and closed the nightstand drawer. Then she went back to her room and began to think about what she was going to take with her to Arizona.

On the way to school the next day, she stopped at the phone booth at the post office. She took the piece of paper out of her pocket, and dialed the numbers. "Collect. Punk." It was ringing. Her father answered. She talked for a while. Then began to cry.

"Are you sure Punk? I don't want to drive up there for you to just change your mind."

"I'm sure Daddy."

"Okay then. Here's what I want you to do. I will call you at school tomorrow, so make sure you go. I don't want you to tell anyone, and don't do anything that makes your mom suspicious. OK?"

"Okay. I love you Daddy."

"Okay Punk," he said laughing. "I'll talk to you tomorrow."

She hung up and went to school. She talked to no one, and no one talked to her. After school she went to bed, refusing to acknowledge the needs of her little brothers and sister.

The next day she received a note asking her to come to the office. She answered the phone, and listened to the instructions. She went back to her locker and got her coat, looked at her notebooks, but took none of them. She left the school building without permission.

She walked home in that February afternoon, wondering what was going to happen in her life now. Of all the bad things she had done, this was definitely the worst. She was running away. At home she packed a brown paper sack with some clothes. She went into the living room and watched out the window. When the brown car drove up to the house, she went out and shut the door. It all felt very final. She got in the car, and they drove away. She felt like she was leaving her entire world behind.

The drive to her father's home in Arizona was uneventful except for the fact that she saw geography that captivated her by its changes. Jimmy said little, smoking cigarettes and drinking coffee. Sometimes she slept. Mostly though, she looked out the window and thought of her sister and brothers she had left behind, feeling distressed. Would they wonder where she had gone? Who would do her chores? What about Harlan and Tony? Who would fix dinner? Would Sissy be okay?

What Punk didn't know was that her mother knew she was going to live with her father in Arizona. Jimmy had called her at the bar. Elizabeth agreed not do anything about it, and was in fact relieved to have her gone. Jimmy agreed not to report Elizabeth for collecting welfare on a child who no longer lived with her.

Seven

What did I dream? I do not know; the fragments fly like chaff

Jimmy was living with Veronica in a two bedroom flat in the small town of Quartzite. He worked as a mechanic at a garage. Veronica worked at the general store. They had a quiet life together. Veronica had moved from New York to get away from her drug habit, meeting Jimmy in the Oregon Timberland. They had stayed together when Jimmy moved to Arizona to dodge child support for his six children.

Veronica tried hard, but was ill suited for the fringe. She had grown up the privileged child of a wealthy couple in Manhattan. She was lost in the West, which was what she wanted.

It was early evening the next day when they arrived in Quartzite. Right before they arrived at his house, Jimmy said to his daughter, "Listen, just so you know, people here don't know I have kids, so don't go saying anything about your brothers and sister. And don't go thinking you can play me for a fool to get an easy ride from me. I didn't have kids so I could go broke spoiling them. Oh, and be nice to Veronica. She's gotten real fat, but she's still okay. Don't say anything about it. Am I clear, Punk?"

"Yes," she said, but she wasn't at all sure what he was talking about. She just knew she was tired, and when they arrived, went in and lay down on a bed. A real bed.

When Veronica came into the kitchen the next morning, Jimmy had already left for work. Punk sat at the little kitchen table eating olives out of the can and a piece of bread.

"Good morning," Veronica said, in a perky, gentle voice.

Punk looked at her. Yes, she was large, but had a nice smile. Her hair was long and shiny. Her eyes were very blue and she wore glasses.

"Hi," Punk said, and went back to spooning the olives from the can and sucking out their juice before eating them. When she was done, she drank the olive juice and threw the can away.

"Um, would you like some cereal or something?"

"That's okay. I didn't know what was okay to eat, so I just had this. I hope its okay."

"Yeah, that's fine, but you can have anything that's here. Okay?"

"Okay."

"Maybe we should talk about school. The nearest middle school is Fender. It's 40 miles away and they have a bus stop here in town. You wanna go over there tomorrow, get a fresh start by enrolling on Monday?"

"No."

"Maybe we should wait a week, and give you a chance to get used to the climate. How does that sound?"

"Okay. I was wondering if I could take a shower."

"Of course! Let me show you where stuff is. What did you bring to wear?" It hadn't escaped Veronica's attention that it looked as if Punk had slept in her overalls.

"Just a few things. I don't know. It's winter in Oregon." The word Oregon sounded so very far away, as if it were the moon. Her thoughts drifted off as Veronica continued to talk about something in the bathroom.

That day and the next went slowly. Veronica noticed Punk would walk around the little flat, watch TV and then go back to bed. Finally, on the afternoon of the fourth day, Veronica asked if she needed to do some laundry, and if she wanted to help with dinner.

"Yeah. Okay," Punk said. She went back to her room and retrieved the brown bag of clothes she had brought. Veronica took them to the hall closet that served as the laundry room. She loaded into the wash three pairs of underwear, two men's western shirts, and a pair of blue jeans.

"Punk, you know what I was thinking? I was thinking maybe a new outfit might help you feel more comfortable about going to school. What do you say about that?"

"Okay. If it's okay with Dad." She hadn't seen her Dad since the night they arrived. He came home after she was asleep and left before she got up. She wondered if everything was still okay.

"I'll talk to him when he gets home tonight. Tomorrow is Saturday, we might be able to find some sales in Blythe. It's just across the river, in California."

"Does Dad always work really late?"

"No." She paused, and said in her same upbeat voice, "He hasn't been working late. He usually goes out after work. Sometimes I go with him. Since you've been here, I thought it would be nice if we got to know each other a little bit. I don't have any children."

"How old are you?"

"Twenty-four. How old are you?"

"Thirteen, but I am going to be 14 in July, so really I am 13 and a half. Can I have a beer? It's Friday night."

"I don't know if that's okay. Is Friday some special night you get to drink beer?"

"Yeah. Sometimes. Not all the time, just whenever it is there."

"Well, I guess one won't hurt. Don't say anything to your Dad though; I don't want to get in trouble with him."

"Me either."

Arizona was a funny place to Punk. No one had heaters. Everyone had air conditioners instead. Funny too, was the river that ran through the town. It was dry and rocky. No water at all, but it had bridges over it. Veronica told her it was called a wash, not a river. That it only has water once a year.

They went into Blythe on Saturday. Jimmy stayed home sleeping. Veronica did most of the talking.

"Maybe we should start with the basics. How about bras and panties? Do you know what size you are? How many pairs do you have?" It had not escaped Veronica that Punk didn't wear a bra, but most definitely needed one.

"I never had a bra. I have four pairs of underwear."

"Okay. Let's do that first. Then we can get a pop and talk about what kind of style you want to wear."

"Style?"

"Yeah, you know, country, trendy?"

"I don't know. I don't really care. Some more underwear and a bra sound good. I like overalls, too. And jeans. And t-shirts. It's really warm here. Oregon has got a lot of snow right now. Everything is all icy. You sit by the woodstove all the time." Once again her mind wandered to her old home. She knew there was nothing there for her, but she was not sure there was anything here either. Except for Veronica, she was nice.

"Great. Now we have a plan."

They shopped all day. On the drive home, Veronica noticed Punk was smiling for the first time since she had arrived. Veronica relaxed. Maybe everything would be okay after all.

It was after seven when they arrived back in Quartzite. Driving down Main Street Veronica saw Jimmy's motorcycle at the tavern.

"Are you hungry? We could stop and have some dinner with your dad. They have chicken and jo-jo's at the tavern."

"Okay." They pulled the Eldorado into the parking lot.

It was the only tavern in town and was always crowded. It had a drive-up window for bottled liquor and cigarettes. Three pool tables placed in a row were at the far end. A jukebox and Packman game were against the wall opposite the long bar. The oversized room was filled with small round tables, each with too many chairs crowding them. It sounded pleasantly noisy to Punk.

Jimmy sat at a table near the bar with two other men. They were drinking beer and watching the TV above the bar.

"Hey, it's the shoppers. Did you get what you needed?" Jimmy, didn't get up, but put his arm around Veronica's waist as they walked up.

"Yea. We worked up an appetite. How about we join you for dinner?"

"Girls, always wanting something. They can't make money worth a damn, but they sure can spend it," Jimmy said laughing to the man sitting next to him. "Earl, James, this is Punk; she's from Oregon, staying with us for a little while."

"Nice to meet you." They both looked at her. Earl was a large man with gray hair. He smiled at her and she could see that he was missing his two front teeth. James was young with dark, neatly trimmed hair. She sat down next to him.

"Earl is my boss, and James here, is trainin' in mechanics down at the shop. You could say he is the gopher." The guys laughed at some joke only they knew. Veronica ordered a rum and coke and bucket of chicken and side of Jo-Jo's. Punk ordered a pop.

She sat uncomfortably for an hour before thinking she wanted to leave, but Veronica was having a good time playing pool with Earl's wife, who had come in looking for Earl. Jimmy was talking and laughing, but she couldn't hear above the noise. It crossed her mind that she should walk home.

The bar began to fill up with the evening crowd. James asked Punk if she knew how to play pool. She did, she said. He asked her if she wanted to play a game. She said she would if he got her a rum and coke. He did. The evening got better for her after that. They all had such a good time that the event was repeated nearly every Saturday night for the next year.

That next week she began school in the town of Fender. She rode the bus an hour each way. She talked to no one. The kids were very different than what she was used to. She had never been around Hispanic, African American, or Asian students, and didn't know how to act. She stayed to herself.

On the bus ride to school during the second week, a Hispanic girl sat next to her, and began a conversation. Her name was Marcella, and she was also in the eighth grade. They talked about a boy who told Marcella he thought Punk was cute.

Punk had no opinion of him, had never noticed him.

"How do you like Arizona? Is school different than Oregon? It's harder isn't it? They say Arizona has the most difficult academic standard in the US."

"It's very different.... you can't wear shorts or sandals to school in Oregon. It's too cold, and the teachers would send you home. Yesterday I saw a girl at school with a bathing suit top on. That just wouldn't go on in Oregon. Lots of other things too. Like there are a lot of niggers. I don't think Oregon has niggers, at least I never saw any. And the music is way different. In Oregon, we are lucky to listen to the radio at home. Here, it seems everyone has his or her own Walkman. I've never even

heard of a Walkman 'til I moved here." She paused and looked at
Marcella, who was starring at her with a look Punk was not sure
how to interpret. Marcella didn't say another word; she just got
up and moved to another seat. Punk wasn't sure what had happened, so she turned back to watching the scenery go by.

During recess Marcella approached her with three other
girls. "Hey, I heard you calling me a nigger. Is that true?"

Punk said nothing. They looked menacing. She knew she
was in trouble, and tried to walk away. One girl stepped in front
of her and gave her a shove.

"Hey! I'm talking to you, white trash from Oregon."

Someone from behind had a hold of her hair, pulling her
head back. "This is what we like to do with white trash, here in
Arizona." A fist struck her jaw. Another landed in the stomach.
She doubled over and fell to her knees. A shoe delivered a blow
to her side. Then a whistle blew.

"Hey, break it up. Go on, get outta here. Mandy, Mandy!
Move it!" Punk looked at the ground. Only a teacher's shoes
were in view. She looked up to see a teacher without a spot of
compassion on her face.

"That's no way to make friends, miss. Go to the restroom
and wash up." She walked away. This is not a good day, Punk
thought.

Everyone handles change differently. Punk withdrew. She
found her only friend in Veronica. When she got off the bus, she
went to the general store where she would find Veronica at the
counter. They would chat, and then she would go back to the flat
and wait for her to get home. If Jimmy came home for dinner,
they would BBQ and drink beer. By the time summer came, and

school let out, Punk was becoming accustomed to the dry desert environment, the strange way of talking, and the different colors of people.

She learned a lot from Veronica. She told Veronica about the fight at school, and Veronica was good for sympathy. Veronica told her about New York and drugs. She helped her figure out how to use a tampon and shave her under arms and legs. Veronica tried to talk to her about sex, but it became uncomfortable, so she changed the subject. Veronica suspected Punk had been abused in some way, but couldn't get her to talk about it. Instead they watched TV. During the hot part of the day, they took naps or read. They shared the same novels.

In July Jimmy gave Punk a motorcycle for her fourteenth birthday. It was a used dirt bike from the garage. She rode endlessly through the dry wash beds, across the desert, and around town. She would stop at her father's garage if she needed fuel, and she always found James willing to keep her company. She went to dinner with him several times, provided he brought her a bottle of wine. It was the best time she had ever had. Even at 112 degrees, Punk wished summer would last forever.

When school started again Punk was a freshman, and she looked more like a person of the desert state. Her skin had baked to a dark chocolate brown, matching her hair and eyes. She felt more confident and relaxed than she had the year before, and she made friends. It was funny she thought, that she didn't want summer to end because it was so nice, but now that she was back in school, it was still nice. Sadly, it wasn't to last.

In high school, students could leave the campus to have lunch. Punk bought cigarettes from the vending machine at the service station. Then she hung out in the school parking lot and drank whatever anyone would share, and smoked. On one of those days, she was called to the principal's office.

He called her in from the small waiting area, and closed the door behind her.

"Have a seat, Ms. Moran."

She sat down across the desk from him. It was such a pretty day. Pleasantly intoxicated, she was happy and relaxed.

"You know, I really don't give a fuck what you drink or smoke. I am trying to run a school. There are students here who don't want to be in a classroom with students who are using drugs and alcohol. That means you and your parking lot friends. Why don't you do us both a favor and not come back to class if you are drunk or high. Got it?" He got up and walked to the door. Opening it, he said, "Goodbye, Ms. Moran."

Confused and shamed by his knowledge of her activities, she went out the door and to her locker. She would have to mellow out, she told herself. The students who reported her were jealous because she was happy. She wasn't like them. They moped around complaining about homework and teachers, and she didn't have a care in the world. She could flunk every class and it wouldn't matter. No one stressing her out. Except the principal, who was a total asshole, and must have a stick up his butt. Yeah, she'd have to mellow out a bit, be more discreet.

Punk was the kind of individual people notice. She had an approachable energy that stood out to other students. This was especially so when she drank, and like her father, had little control over her mouth. Right before Christmas break, she was expelled from school for two weeks.

During that time Veronica moved out. She told Punk it was because her dad was a jackass, and Jimmy said it was because Veronica was fat. The house was empty without her. There was no food, no one to talk to, and Punk realized that things were not going so well. Christmas had no tree or gifts. Her motorcycle had been taken away. That was her gift to him, her father said with a laugh. She didn't find anything he ever said to be funny.

One night her father came home drunk. She was sitting on the sofa watching Dukes of Hazard, when he sat down beside her. "Look," he slurred, "I know you miss Veronica. I want you to know though, that you can come to me for anything. I will help you however I can." He put his hand on her thigh. She looked at his face, his glassy eyes, his breath smelled like canned dog food. "I can answer any questions you have, even about sex." He stroked her thigh. "I know a lot more than you might think. I am here for you if you want it."

Punk's stomach rolled. She got up and went to her room. She locked the door, and took the bottle of Bacardi out from her top drawer. What was that about? She thought. Did that really happen?

On her second day back to school, she was called into the principal's office. This time a secretary was in the room with them.

He looked at her with unconcealed rage. "Ms. Moran, I am expelling you from school for another two weeks. That's all the law will allow. If you choose not to come back after your two weeks are up, that's okay too. Good-bye now." He opened the door and motioned her out. She was not surprised this time. School was a waste of time. Everything was a waste of time.

When she got off the bus, she went to the store where Veronica worked. Veronica was at the counter ringing up a customer. Veronica looked at her. "The school called me. I told them I would speak with your dad." The customer left, and she came around and hugged Punk. "Punk, I want you to come to my trailer on Sunday around 9:30. Okay. We will talk more then."

At home, the house was empty. She went to her room and locked the door. The next morning she began vomiting, all day and all night. She drank water and slept. Her father would pound on the door in the evening. "You can come out now. I won't hurt you." But she didn't, except to use the bathroom and vomit.

It was Sunday. Her stomach hurt and she was tired. She drank some water, got dressed and walked to Veronica's trailer. The neighborhood had little rock gardens between the trailers, and palm trees in the center, like a park. Even though it was February, it wasn't cold. It's funny she thought, Veronica doesn't usually get up this early on Sunday.

When she arrived, Veronica was still in bed. Punk sat on the edge of the bed and they talked. "Please don't be upset with me, but I want you to go to the AA meeting that's here in the park. It starts at 10." She paused, trying to read the teenager's face, but it was blank. "Hey, you get free coffee." She let out a sigh. "Just try and think of maybe changing some things that will make your life better." Veronica put her arms around her and hugged tightly. "I just don't want to see you grow up to be like your dad."

Punk stiffened. "I will never be like him."

"I don't mean you, I mean your life. You deserve a chance for a better life. Please do this for me. Please?"

Punk got up and went out without saying goodbye. She lit a Marlboro and walked over to the laundry facility. On the door was a sign that said 'AA meeting here today 10-11.' Inside she could see several old people sitting in a waiting area of the room, drinking from styrofoam cups. On the clothes counter was a coffee pot, and a stack of cups. Stacks of brochures were set out where you fold your clothes. Before she could walk on past, a woman appeared behind her and opened the door.

"Welcome," the woman said in a quiet, somber voice, and held the door open for her. Without realizing it, Punk stepped inside and attended her first AA meeting.

Only five people were there, and they sat in a small circle, so close together, their knees touched. They were old people wearing weathered faces. Punk sat quietly as they took turns reading from a book. Each time a person spoke, they introduced themselves and said they were an alcoholic, even if they had already spoken earlier. It seemed like a very important secret meeting, and they seemed so serious that despite her discomfort, she sat still.

As the meeting was ending, the woman who opened the door for her asked if she would like to share anything.

Punk didn't introduce herself. No way was she going to be on some government list of alcoholics. "I got expelled from school for drinking. You see, it's the only thing that makes me happy, you know. I feel okay, even when I know that it's not okay, I don't care."

The woman who had opened the door for her replied to this in a quiet voice. "It doesn't have to be that way. You can make changes through this program that will help to make life on life's term's better. You don't have to drink ever again if you don't want to."

Punk felt the weight of her hopelessness crash over her like a wave. She did not come to this meeting to defend herself. "Oh really? I can make changes. Really. Like what? What do I have any power over in my life? I don't even have a say over whether

I will eat today, where I will sleep. I'm not like you. Free to live and be around who ever you want. That won't happen for me."

Two people began to talk at once, and Punk hung her head. She felt dizzy and nauseous and wanted to run. She began to cry. "And I am so sick."

Suddenly, it got quiet. Then the woman asked her, "What can I do to help?"

"There is nothing anyone can do," Punk replied.

"Do you need to see a doctor, go to the clinic? I could take you to a clinic in Blythe and you could see a nurse."

Everyone was looking at her, but she held her gaze on this woman. She stared back at her and said, "Yes."

"We can go tomorrow. I can come by and pick you up, okay?"

"Okay." Then they all held hands in a circle, and chanted an undistinguishable prayer. Punk felt relief, but she didn't know why.

The next morning, just like she had said, the woman came and picked her up. They drove in silence, until she said, "Punk, is that your real name?"

"No, it's my nickname."

"What's your real name?"

"Lena."

"May I call you Lena?"

"Ok."

The clinic was crowded. She was called in to pee in a cup, then returned to the waiting room.

"Ms. Moran," the nurse called to her. Punk's heart jumped. She walked up to the nurse's window. "You are sick because you are pregnant."

Stunned, she stood there.

"Did you come with someone you would like me to talk to?"

"Yes. She's in the waiting room." They walked out together.

"Hi." The nurse shook the woman's hand. "Lena is sick because she is pregnant. Do you want to schedule an abortion at this time?"

"No, NO! Thank you for your help. Let's go Lena." She took Lena's hand and led her through the busy waiting room, and out the front door.

They just sat in the car in silence. Then, in a rare moment of emotion, Lena put her face in her hands and began to cry.

"I can't be pregnant. I can't be pregnant." She repeated over and over. The woman in the drivers seat just sat there and let her cry. When Lena had stopped mumbling, she handed her a tissue.

"It's going to be okay. Let's focus on today." Lena looked at her and blew her nose.

"I can't be pregnant. My father is going to kill me." She began to sob again.

"Hey, I'm hungry. It's lunchtime. Let's go to McDonald's and get something to eat. We will be able to think better when our stomach's aren't growling."

Lena sobbed as they drove. They ate burgers and drank coke in the car. After eating, Lena got out and threw up in the trashcan by the front door. People stared out the window of the restaurant. When she got back in the car, they drove to a park. The tears had dried up, and she drank her pop and smoked a cigarette.

"What am I going to do?"

"Do you know who the father is?"

"No," Lena lied.

"You don't have to have an abortion. There are people who will help you and adopt the baby."

"There is no way Dad is going to let me live after he finds out. He is going to kill me."

"I won't let him kill you," she said. She was skeptical about the drama. It was probably just the normal fear some parents instill in their children to keep them from misbehaving. Still, she felt uneasy.

"Well, I just want you to know that you don't have to go through this alone. You are not alone. Do you hear what I am saying? You are not alone. You don't have to do this alone."

Lena laid her head on the woman's shoulder and closed her eyes. She was so tired.

Three hours passed before she opened her eyes. She was lying on the front seat of the car. The woman was sitting on a bench in the park. When she saw Lena sitting up, she got up and got back in the car.

"How are you feeling?" she asked. Lena looked dazed.

"What happened?"

"Nothing happened. You fell asleep. Are you ready to go?"

There was no response from the passenger seat. She started the car and pulled away from the park. They had to go back sometime.

Go where? Lena asked herself. Home? There is no such place. There never was. She felt empty and numb.

The day's experience was surreal for Lena. Ordinary kindness is not expected or reasonable in the fringe. The thought of a stranger knowing about her immoral problem, and continuing to spend time with her was a confusing contradiction. Lena didn't believe people could behave that way.

"Lena," the woman said, as they drove into Quartzite. "You've got to tell your dad."

"No." Lena paused. "I am going to go ......somewhere. I don't know where, but I am going. I need some money. Do you have any money?"

"I can't give you money. Running away will not help. I swear that's the truth. You have to tell your dad, and he will find you help."

Lena looked at the woman. "You have no idea what you are saying. It doesn't work that way. He is not going to help me. I can't tell him. He can find out after I leave."

"What about if I was there while you told him." She looked at Lena. "Would that be better?"

"No. I can't tell him. It is better for me to go somewhere. Anywhere. This is the last thing Dad is going to want in his life. He will kill me, cut me up in little pieces and put me out with the trash."

"Okay. I understand what you're saying, but adults know that sometimes they have to do difficult things. Once he gets over the shock, he will help. Even if it is just to find you medical care. He will. What if I told him? How would you feel about that?"

"Maybe. I don't know. You would do that?"

"Yeah. You could just sit and let me do the talking."

"No. I said I couldn't be there when he finds out."

"Are you ok with me telling him?"

"Yeah. I think that would be okay. Then he can think, plan how to get rid of me, instead of just chopping me up." Through the now- dark car, she gave a small laugh. The woman laughed, too. Lena had a sinking feeling about this.

The woman dropped her off at the dark house. She said she would go to the tavern where her father was. Lena went inside, took off her shoes and went to bed fully dressed. She pulled the light blanket over her head and closed her eyes. If she concentrated hard enough, she might be able to disappear from reality.

As the woman drove to the tavern and parked she prayed. "God, grant me the serenity to accept the things I cannot change, the courage to change the things I can, and the wisdom to know the difference." Then she went inside.

Sitting at a table with several other men and a young blonde, Jimmy was clearly intoxicated. She walked up to him and asked if he was Jimmy Moran.

"Yes," he said, "unless you're the IRS. Then I'm John Smith." He laughed at his joke.

"May I speak with you privately?"

"About what?" He slurred.

"It's about your daughter."

"And you are..."

"I'm just a friend."

"Well, 'just- a- friend,' I ain't movin' unless I gotta take a piss, and I ain't gotta piss, so whatever ya gotta say, I don't wan- na hear it."

The woman just stood there. The table had gone silent. "Maybe it's important Jimmy," the blonde girl said.

"Yeah, okay. Don't just stand there. Say whatever ya gotta say."

The woman looked at the other occupants at the table. Jimmy was the most visibly drunk. The rest sat stone faced, waiting for an ax to fall.

"I took your daughter to the clinic in Blythe today. She's pregnant."

"What!" He yelled and jumped to his feet tipping his chair over. Jimmy looked at her in disbelief that quickly turned to rage.

"That fucking whore. What are you, a whore friend?"

The woman took a step back as Jimmy got in her face.

"Don't talk to me that way. If she were a whore, which she is not, it would be because that's all she knows. But she's not a whore. She needs her father to help her. She doesn't need to be punished."

"What the *fuck* do *you* know about my family?" he bellowed.

"Okay Jimmy, calm down. Just calm down, it's not her fault. She's just the bearer of bad news." Earl stood up expecting Jimmy to try and grab her.

But Jimmy didn't sit down. He got back in her face and said; "Don't think *you* can tell *me* about my daughter. I know what she is. Oh, I'll help her all right. I'll help her right out onto the street. I've had enough of her bullshit. Never going to school, drunk all the time. She's probably slept with the whole town."

The woman summoned the last of her words. "She is exactly what you have brought her up to be. If you wanted her to have a different life, you should have provided a different home." It was the best she could do in the heat of the moment.

She turned and left the tavern, shaking and feeling ill. "God," she said, "I really don't like practicing alcoholics. You're in charge now. I did what you asked. Please watch over Lena. Thank you, God."

God was with Lena, because Jimmy didn't cut her up in pieces and put her out with the trash. He didn't bother knocking on her door either. When he got to her locked door, he threw all his weight against it several times before the wood gave way. In his hand he held a bag of Doritos. He continued to shove chips in his mouth, as he sat on the edge of Lena's bed. She was hiding like a small child, under the covers.

"Hey. Wake up." He made a fist and rapped on her head as if it were a door.

She sat up and looked at him. He was sloppy drunk, eating Doritos and laughing at himself. She moved to the corner of the bed, as far as she could get from him. "Hey. Guess what? A lady friend of yours came into the bar tonight and humiliated me in front of my friends." Chunks of Doritos flew out of his mouth when he slurred the word "humiliated."

"Yeah. She said you are pregnant." He was laughing now. "Yeah. Just like that. In front of everyone." He stopped laughing.

"You fucking bitch!" he yelled, and lunged across the bed, and began to strike the top of her head. Lena covered her head with her arms to defend herself from the blows he kept trying to deliver to her face. His drunken rage prevented him from hitting his mark.

"I'm sorry. I'm sorry," Lena kept saying over and over again.

He stopped pounding on her. "Ya're sorry? Ya're sorry? What's that? What's that ya're sayin'? Sorry ain't nothin'!" he slurred.

She lowered her arms. "I didn't mean for this to happen. I am sorry." She was sobbing.

He looked at her. The room was dark, but he could still see her face, and it made him angry just to look at her. He leaned toward her, and spit in her face. "I hope you die in your own shit. Then you'll be sorry. You fucking whore!" and he spat Doritos on her again.

He turned around and walked out of her room. She was covered in half chewed pieces of Doritos. If it were possible to will her own death, she would have died a thousand times. Only God knew she wasn't going to die.

Veronica showed up at the bus station to hug her goodbye. Jimmy was there with the blonde lady from the bar. Lena hugged Veronica.

"Do you have any money to eat on? It's a long way to Oregon."

"No, but it's okay."

"Here, and she put a ten in her hand. Be careful. I feel really bad for you right now, but I know you're going to be okay." She said these words to sooth herself. She didn't look at Lena, because she was afraid Lena would see she was lying.

Lena looked out the window as the bus began to move. Veronica was waving, but Jimmy had turned his back and was walking away, his arm around his new blonde.

For three days and two nights she rode the bus. She arrived at the Barberton bus depot in the early morning hours. It was a frozen February; she had been gone exactly one year.

Eight

For want of a nail, the shoe was lost. For want of a shoe, the horse was lost.

She pulled the address out of her pocket. Barberton was a big town. Well, bigger than she had ever lived in before. Having never been there, with no phone number to call, she walked through the empty and dark town, looking for Chuckanut Street. Her mother had moved the family to Barberton in the summer. She wasn't sure why. She would ask Jean, if she didn't freeze to death first. She slung her duffle bag over her shoulder and kept walking. Shortly she came to Pinecone, then Chestnut. She hoped she was going in the right direction. Then she came to Chuckanut. Relieved, she went down the street until she came to the address that matched the piece of paper. It was a large white weathered house with a sagging roof and porch.

Numb from the cold, she went through the unlocked front door without knocking. No one was awake yet. The clock on the wall said 6:50. She went through the entrance and lay down on the sofa using her duffle bag for a pillow, but sleep did not come. She wasn't even sure the people in the house were expecting her. She was cold, tired and sick. Lena was fifteen and pregnant, she didn't belong in the adult world, nor was she a child.

The house that was her new home was in a forgotten area of town. It was an old drafty box built in the 1940's. When you entered the front door, you entered into a large empty parlor. It had tall narrow windows and a cold hardwood floor. The walls were a dirty gray, and the windows were naked. A door to the right went to a small room, which served as Jean's bedroom. Lena would share a single bed with her sister.

Through the parlor was what used to be known as a sitting room. It was a much smaller room with a fireplace and carpeted area. This is where the Moran family spent its time. A TV sat on an end table against a wall with its rabbit ear antenna flopped to one side. A tapestry of a mountain goat hung over the long narrow window, and two shabby couches crowded the remaining space.

The kitchen entry was to the right of the sitting room. In it was a small table, a refrigerator and stove. The sink held the dirty dishes, and the counter held the clean dishes no one ever put away. The kitchen was the main sleeping area for the dogs. Elizabeth fed them leftover oatmeal with gravy in the mornings. During the day, they were let out to roam the neighborhood until someone came home from school.

On the other side of the sitting room was a stairway leading to the rooms upstairs. This was the travel path for the boys in the family. Lena and Jean never went up there. There was one small bathroom between the kitchen and living, and it was always being used. Jean told her they moved to Barberton after Gary found out Elizabeth hadn't actually divorced their Dad. Gary had gotten so mad he threw them out of the house, and Elizabeth moved them to Barberton so she could get work.

At first, Lena just slept. When she did come out of the bedroom, she wandered around in a kind of emotional shock. She wasn't required to go to school, and no one asked her any questions. On the ninth day of being there, Elizabeth came into her room and told her she was going to the clinic that morning, and again the next morning. She didn't ask why. She knew why. She was sure everyone on the planet knew about her, and that she better just do what she was told to do.

The drive to the clinic was long. The little pickup truck entered the freeway at 40 miles an hour, and reached its final speed of 45. Elizabeth tried to engage Lena in conversation about anything other than what they were going to face. But Lena ignored her, choosing instead to listen for Ellen. While Lena looked out the window at the dirty March snow, Ellen began reciting a list of intolerable experiences that had led to this day.

Ellen, the voice in Lena's head that had been born out of childhood necessity years earlier, chatted about the filthy nature of life, and the upcoming tragic events that would follow her to the end of her days. Ellen raged about her obvious desolate future, and the powerlessness over changing it. "If only you could get you out of here," Ellen kept saying. But those statements in her head were useless. Ellen provided solutions without the means to attain them.

Elizabeth was also trying to make conversation. Not getting a response from her efforts with small talk, Elizabeth took a courageous leap and began to talk about how this was the best thing for her, for everyone. Still, Lena said nothing. Knowing the unpredictable nature of her first daughter, she said, "don't make this worse than it is. If you say anything about not wanting this, you won't live long enough to regret it. I have never been the one to tell you what is what, but I will now. No surprises today. I mean that Punk."

The clinic was in a small building just over the Snake River in Idaho. Lena didn't know about the abortion laws, she didn't know much at all about what was happening, so she just kept her mouth shut.

The first appointment at the clinic involved paperwork, and a nurse explaining the procedure. Elizabeth stayed with her the entire time. When they were done talking about how Lena could change her mind at any time, for any reason, she was asked to get undressed and lay on the table.

The next day the drive was the same, except Elizabeth played the radio and sang to country songs. Lena looked out the window and watched the dirty patches of snow go by. She tried to will herself to die, but her internal guardian told her to hang on. It would all be over soon enough. So she hung on. And when the doctor came in and sucked out the baby, she didn't say a word. She didn't change her mind, or cry, or ask for pain medication. She just hung on.

Nine

Vintery, mintery, cutery, corn,
apple seed and apple thorn;

It took a month to come out of the shock of the abortion. It was April in Barberton, and the crab apple trees in the front yard were beginning to bud. Lena tried to ignore the comments from Elizabeth that she needed to go back to school. Then one day, out of boredom and curiosity, Lena got up, showered, and walked to the high school. It only lasted a month, but it was what she needed to do at the time.

The school was crowded and noisy. Both Web and Lee were well known for their participation in sports. Web had graduated, but hung out to sell drugs. They pretended not to know her, and she pretended to be no one. They were the stars of both football and basketball. Web had left her alone for the past two months, and for that she was grateful. Lena believed it was because he felt sorry for her.

Ellen believed Web was waiting for his chance to pound her again.

That chance came on a Friday night. Elizabeth had left for the weekend with Ron or Rob or someone like that. Jean and Lena made dinner out of boxed macaroni and cheese. Jean came into the kitchen with a food chart she had been given at school, and said they had to serve vegetables. Lena opened a can of green beans and set it on the table. Harlan and Tony wouldn't leave the TV so Jean took them plates of food into the living room.

It was kind of nice being in charge, Lena thought. Then Web and Lee came home. They brought with them two scabby looking guys, all glassy eyed and stoned. They started eating the food out of the pan, all four of them laughing and carrying on. Lena and Jean went to their room and locked the door. Jean crawled under the bed, and Lena sat on the bed, defiantly staring at the door. She could feel the rage rising up, threatening to take over her entire body. She wanted to kill someone. She wanted to rip the red hair off Web's scalp and shove it in his mouth. She was envisioning stabbing his green eyes with a fork, and then pulling them out, leaving bloody sockets behind. Jean just wanted the night to be over.

After a brief quiet, Lena heard him at the door.

"Hey Punk, open the door. Guy wants to see you. Come out and meet my friends."

Lena froze. The sound of his kindness was like vomit served as pudding, filthy.

He began to pound on the door. "Hey, I know you are in there. Open the fucking door. Open the door Punk, or I will break it down." He pounded even harder.

"Hey man, maybe they left." Lee said. "Don't break the door. Mom 'll kill us."

But he didn't stop. Jean whimpered under the bed. Lena whispered, "I am going to go out the window. Come on."

"No, its cold." She was crying. "I want Mommy. Go get Mommy."

"I don't know where she is." She thought for a moment. "Okay. I'll go find her. Just close the window and stay in the room."

Lena went to the long narrow window that went outside. She quietly slid it open. It was dark. Jean came out from under the bed, as Lena jumped to the ground. They didn't look at each other as Jean closed the window and Lena ran away. It was better not to look too long.

She ran the length of the town to the Idle Hour Tavern. All the while Ellen was saying, "just keep running. Never look back. Don't stop until you get somewhere else." But she knew she couldn't just leave Jean, Tony or Harlan like that. Not again. So she stopped running when she arrived at the parking lot full of pickup trucks. She coolly stepped into the dark and noisy bar and let the door close behind her. It felt like a cave. Cave with animals. She wanted to run, but she had a duty.

Lena looked around the neon lit room. A long bar stretched to the left and tables crowed together in the rest of the room. No one greeted her, and she stepped to the side to let a man pass by. She spotted her mother easily, at a table with two men and another woman. They were laughing. She looks happy, Lena thought.

She walked up to the table. "Mom, can you come home? Jean wants you."

"Punk, what are you doing here? Oh, Jim, this is Punk. What's wrong honey? I told you to stay at home."

"Mom, Web has some friends over, they were pounding on the door. They won't leave us alone. Can you come home and tell them to leave?"

"No. I think you are big enough to tell them yourself. You are always so dramatic about these kind of things." Her mother's eyes were laughing.

"I really neeeeeed you to come home now. Jean is crying. They ate the boy's dinner. They won't leave us alone." Her words came fast with a kind of little girl whine.

"Ok honey, I will be home in a little while. Why don't you go on and tell Jean I will be right there."

Lena looked at the faces around the table. They were looking back at her with patronizing amusement. Lena felt the humiliation begin to rise in her face. She turned and walked briskly out the door, letting it slam behind her.

On the walk home Ellen, friend and internal guardian, talked to her. This time Lena tried to listen.

"Aren't you tired of this? You beg your mother to help, like you have always done, and she laughs at you. She doesn't care, Lena. You need to stop asking her for help, and help yourself. Nothing is going to change unless you change it."

Lena listened and thought. Maybe Ellen was right. But she wasn't sure what she could do. She needed money. She wanted to get back on the bus that brought her to this dirty cold town. If she went back to Arizona, she was sure she could find someone she knew there, someone who would help her.

When she arrived back at the house on Chuckanut Street, it appeared deserted. Inside the house was dark except for the TV Harlan and Tony were watching. She went to her room, the door was unlocked. Jean was in bed, lying quietly holding her bear. They looked at each other.

"Mom will be home in a little while," Lena said. Jean just stared back at her. Lena closed the door. She went into the kitchen, took a bottle of cheap wine out of the refrigerator, and poured herself a glass. She lit a cigarette, and then picked up the phone. She had met a girl at school. She couldn't remember her last name. Sarah something. She said to call her sometime and gave Lena a scrap of paper with a phone number on it.

But Sarah wasn't home. "On a date," Mrs. Winslow said, introducing herself

Desperate, Lena talked to Mrs. Winslow. Crying on the phone, Lena asked if Sarah could call her in the morning. Mrs. Winslow was used to tragedy of the teenage nature. She wasn't sure what was really going on in the girl's life, but she let her talk. When she realized that nothing the girl was saying made sense, that perhaps she had been drinking or something worse. She suggested that she could call back in the morning. Lena hung up and sat in the kitchen by herself, trying to think her way into a better life. But nothing came into her mind.

Eventually the bottle of wine was gone. Her mother had not arrived, and the clock said 1:30. The house was cold. She had been sitting for several hours listening to that voice in her head, and she was stiff and cold. She walked through the living room. Harlan and Tony were sleeping on the sofa. She covered them up and went to the bed she shared with Jean.

The next day Lena left home. She was three months away from turning 16 years old. She felt like she had been hit by a train, and had unfortunately survived. For the second time in her life, she walked away from her home. There was only slight drama involved. She got dressed the next morning, packed a few items into her backpack. She went into the kitchen where Elizabeth was sipping coffee.

"I can't stay here. You said you were coming home last night."

"I did honey. And was there any problem at all? You are so dramatic. What am I supposed to do when you always dramatize everything; I never know what's real and what's not."

"If you were here, you wouldn't have to guess what really is going on, Mom."

They stared at each other momentarily.

"What is it Punk? What do you want?"

Frustrated by the question, Lena simply said, "Whatever. I am not staying. All I do is wait for you to show up and yell at me for something that is not done, something you could be doing if you weren't at the bar."

"Hey, don't talk to me that way. I work hard. You don't see how hard I work. You don't know what it's like trying to make ends meet, paying the bills for this family."

"This isn't a family. I don't know what a family is, but this isn't it. I didn't ask to have kids, but that's what I do. While my friends are out at the movies, I baby sit for you so you can go to the bar. I am not doing this anymore." She turned around only to be grabbed by the arm.

"Hey, where do you think you are going? You don't get to say where you go and what you do. I say! I am your mother and you will do what I ask you to do!"

"Not anymore!" Lena paused and said slowly, quietly, "I don't want to help you with your life, and you don't have anything that will help me with mine. I know I can do a better job with my own life. I don't know what I am going to do, but it will be better than this. I'm leaving."

"No, you are not! Where would you go? You have no one. Nooothinng!"

Lena knew this. She replied to this statement with the only answer she had. "Yes, I know. But I'm leaving anyway. I don't know where I am going, but I'm not going to live here another day. I'll take my chances with life. What's the difference? At least I will be choosing for myself." Lena could see the confusion on Elizabeth face. Then it turned to hurt.

"After everything I have done for you. I gave you a house to sleep in, clothes from my own closet, money when you needed it. You are the most ungrateful, selfish, inconsiderate bitch. I can't believe you are my daughter. It's like you have no loyalty or sense of obligation at all, Punk!"

"My name is Lena, and I didn't ask to be born. If this house is the only choice for me, I'll live in the park. It's not a safe place for me. Web and Lee sell drugs out of the house and Jean and I have to stay in our room with the door locked when you are not home."

"What do you mean by that?"

"You know what I mean. They are constantly trying to put their hands down our pants or squeeze our breasts. Last night they had friends with them...pounding on our door, demanding I come out. I asked you to come home....you don't believe me when I say we need you home. I'm done Mom. I won't live in the same house with them ever again."

"I didn't know..."

"Yes you did!" Lena shot back angrily. "You have known since I was six years old that Web beats me, spits on me, and tries to have sex with me. Remember what you told me? You said, 'Don't let him do that.' Well, I don't know how to keep him from doing that other than to leave. So don't tell me you don't know.... You don't want to know! Maybe Jean doesn't tell you what is going on, but I have. Now I am done. All you have ever done is tell him to be nice. I'm done with how you handle life. I'd rather live on the street and take my chances."

Teenage daughters have a way of showing their mothers a reality that strips away self-delusion. Teenage daughters have a way of cutting through the lies adult women surround themselves with in order to continue in the direction they have set. Elizabeth had her life ahead of her, and she was getting on with it. That meant being the woman she wanted to be. Before anything else, Elizabeth was and always would be, a man's woman. Lena's words were too much reality, too early in the morning. She simply could not deal with the facts of her life as seen through the eyes of an angry teenager.

"Fine." Her mother's lips turned thin and hard. "You're wearing my shoes. Take them off and leave them here."

Without hesitation Lena slipped off the white sneakers. She had no socks underneath. She picked up her bag. She couldn't handle saying goodbye to her sissy, so she just walked through the house and out the front door. It was spring, and the sun was shining. Barefoot, homeless, penniless, she walked down the street, scared but free.

Ten

Rain on the grass, rain on the tree

Spring Gulch Youth Ranch was where they sent kids who had offended the public, their families, or were just plain confused about life. It was the perfect place for Lena, except she hated it, as did all the youth there. In fact, hate was a prerequisite to admission, as was fear. You had to have enough fear and hate in order to stay.

Funded by taxpayers, Spring Gulch rested in a ravine 50 miles away from any community. It was an abandoned forest service station. It had two dormitories, a meal house, a small school building, a recreation building and a singlewide trailer used for administration and counseling. The entire complex was so close together; it could fit into a parking lot. Its only redeeming quality for the students was that there were no fences or gates surrounding the quasi-incarceration facility.

The two dormitories were identical. On the first floor was the community room and showers; on the second floor was the sleeping quarters and a small office. Each dorm slept 18. Separating the girl's dorm from the boy's dorm was a rose garden.

Spring Gulch Youth Ranch was almost as far away from Barberton as you could get without leaving Oregon. The case manager assigned to her by Family Services somehow found the money to send her, and before her summer on the street was over; Lena was a resident at the ranch.

To Lena, as to the rest of the residents at the ranch, it was safe, but lonely. There were always staff to talk to, and a strict schedule of meals, chores and school. The only free time was an hour and a half in the late afternoon, if they had all their class work had been completed. The time could be used for reading or sleeping or extra chores. Chores were considered work, and residents got paid for them. The pay ranged from $0.25 to $1.25 per chore. There were always someone else's chores you could do to make additional money.

Saturdays were the best day of the week at the ranch. The residents got paid for their work, and they loaded up into the bus and went to the country store to spend their money. In 1982, you could buy cigarettes even if you were under eighteen. That's where most of Lena's money went. The rest went to candy. The Ranch paid for everything else the residents needed.

It sounded like a reasonable place from an outside perspective. It was the kind of soft incarceration and rehabilitation expected from an advanced culture. The youth at the ranch didn't think of it in those terms. To them, it was a last ditch effort on their parents' part to get them to straighten up and fly right. The focus was on self-improvement through counseling and discipline. (That would be a teenager's worst idea of living.) Residents arrived with no privileges or privacy. Small privileges were earned slowly through 'step' work. The 'steps' were four levels of responsibility and privileges. Residents were graded on everything from group participation, chores and school attendance to personal hygiene. The steps allowed the students to advance from being under constant supervision, to having a private sleeping room and home passes, for those who could go home.

It was the first time Lena had the time to stop and think since she left the cabin in Silver Lake. She didn't think she was lucky to be there or that it was going to be a good experience. She had made up her mind that if she was going to have any happiness at all, it was going to have to be of her own making. Spring Gulch Ranch was not her idea of improvement. She had no idea what she was going to do, but she was sure this was not it. Most of all, Lena was angry.

On Thursday afternoons, Lena saw Ms. Carol in the counseling office. It was the only time youth were allowed in the building. It was a small, singlewide trailer stationed in the middle of the complex. It was the most modern of the buildings. It had heating in the winter, air conditioning in the summer, mauve colored carpets and blinds. The kitchen had been removed and was filled with locked filing cabinetry. Labels on the outside of the cabinets spelled out their contents: Medical Supplies, Intake Forms, Board Certificates, Personnel, Charge Reports, etc.

It was the beginning of the fourth month of her time at Spring Gulch. Lena sat comfortably in the chair across the desk from Carol. It was rumored that during the fourth month residents move up in the steps. In anticipation of her change in status, Lena confidently smiled.

Carol looked down at Lena's file lying open in front of her, and then turned her stare on the girl across the desk.

"Okay Lena, it's time to cut the crap."

"What?"

"You heard me. You've been here three months. You are a model citizen at our ranch. That tells me you are just waiting it out. You are here to work on your issues. Let's get to them."

"What issues would that be Ms. Carol?"

"Your birth family's abuse and neglect, your abuse of drugs and alcohol, your manipulation of boys, and your secret life. How does that sound to you?" She paused. "I am not moving you up to step three as long as you continue to pretend you are okay. You are not okay."

She was baiting Lena, looking for any emotion that was different from the plastic smile she always wore.

Disappointment, shame, confusion, all brought emotion to the surface and Lena felt the heat rise in her face. Caught completely off guard by the reference to her family, she swallowed the lump in her throat. "Ok *Mssss.* Carol," Lena said sarcastically. "You want to talk about the past, you go first."

"What?" Carol questioned.

"Tell me about your past. Your childhood, what made you choose to work with teenagers who hate you. What make you want to work with kids no one else wants, in a place removed from the rest of the planet. Is it the money? What happened in your past that made you choose to make money watching over kids who detest the very sound of your name? What's that word? Masochism? Maybe you have poor self esteem, and you don't believe you deserve anything better? Maybe you can't get a job anywhere else. Is that what it is?" She took a breath, and folded her hands in front of her. Slowly, in a patronizing voice Lena finished with, "how does that make you feeeeeel?"

Carol sat looking at the smug juvenile face. "Ohhhhhh." She smiled. "So you do have a guardian in there after all."

"What?"

"Haven't you ever noticed that you have a guardian who comes out when you feel pushed around?"

Silence. Lena's mind raced forward, looking for an opening in the trap. She found it. "So you admit to verbally harassing me. Is that the kind of council I am going to be receiving, because I have the right to refuse to participate in something I feel is abusive or disrespectful. I read the handbook. I know my rights."

"Maybe I should have said it differently. What I mean, Lena........ Is when you are backed into a corner, another aspect of your personality comes out to defend you."

"No, I think you were right the first time. Verbally pushing me around is not something I am going to put up with."

Silence.

Carol let out a sigh. It had been a long day. She was wondering if she cut the appointment short, and wrote the girl up for being uncooperative, could she get to the health club before the early rush? She decided she could.

"Well, here's the *deal*. You are not going to be moved up to level three until you begin to work on your issues. You are manipulative, secretive, and very phony. You can talk to me," she paused, "or you can keep a daily journal and submit that instead of face-to-face meetings. It's up to you. Goodbye."

"I don't understand." Lena's voice went soft. "That part of my life is over. I am not that person. I do what I am supposed to here, and still that's not good enough. How can I prove to you that I am a changed person? You set the rules, I follow them, and still I have to stay at level two. Why even have the steps if I can't move up in them? What do I have to say?"

"I think that is all today, Lena. Let me know what you choose to do."

Lena stared at her, then abruptly left the building, angry and confused. Disappointment came out in tears as she hurried to the dorm to write. That was the last face-to-face meeting she was to have with Carol. She wrote in her journal all the immaterial, juvenile attitudes that she saw from the other girls in the dorm. A month later, the night attendant delivered the news. She had achieved step three, and was on her way out.

A few more months and Lena would graduate, but not before she met the middle class and was saved by Jesus.

Eleven

Humpty-Dumpty sat on a wall,
Humpty-Dumpty had a great fall.

The Bakers were an upper middle class couple in their lei-
sure years. They'd reached the time when the children
were grown and educated and had families of there own.
Unfortunately, like many families, they had a straggler: a hang-
er-on who can't seem to leave the nest for a life of their own
making. The one child out of three that is aimless. In the Baker
family, the adult child at home was Janet. She came along at the
very end of Madeline and George's child-rearing years. She was
a surprise. They raised her, as they had the others, in the tradition
of the Heritage Church.

In the Heritage Church, there are four classes of members. At
the bottom are the sinners. They are the misguided followers, the
leaches of the congregation. They consist mainly of the friends
and families of church members. They have lost their way and
somehow made a stop at the church. For whatever reason, they
hang on for a while, sucking up to the other members for advice,
jobs, dates and social engagement.

The next class of church members is the students. They are
called students because they study the bible as a way of life. The
student class is the 'newly delivered unto Jesus' group. They are
the most welcome, most important, most coddled group. Made
up of people who had been witnessed to and become believers,
they attend church like freshman at a university campus. They

are fresh from the world of sin; beautiful and delicate. Some don't survive a season; some grow and join the congregation.

The congregation is the core set of people who act faithfully, religiously, and seek to follow the church's directions. There is no room for misgivings in this class. Second from the top, and the largest group, they vote, give of their finances, and obey according to the directions of the masters.

The masters, or the first class, are the honored, righteous leaders. The masters are above all else, the deliverers of the spiritual guidance as directed by the Book of Life. Not just ordinary men, masters hold God's special certification, Doctor's of Religious Philosophy. You find the masters in the church board, conference board, and world board. They take their sacred jobs very seriously. These few men are the transparent door keepers. They hold the keys to the house and home. They decide on the moral level, all that is sacred in the home, and how that sacredness will be protected and transferred to the next generation.

The Bakers household had generations of participation in the masters. If it were not for Janet Baker being a girl, and being a sinner, she too would be a part of this significant group.

But Janet was a sinner. Not flagrantly, she didn't create a show of it. She knew better than that. She valued being invited to the best parties and round table functions too much to display her lustful heart. She did her best to keep her secret life separate from her spiritual life.

It so happened that one of Madeline's community duties was to sit on the board of directors for Spring Gulch. Someone had to, after all, look after the souls of the fallen youth. And when it was time for Lena to start taking home visits, and no home was available, it was Madeline's duty to take her home with her. It was Madeline's duty to take her to church. It was Madeline's duty to save her soul for Jesus.

Lena had been given weekend passes to attend church with the Baker family. It was like manna from heaven. The Baker's were generous with Lena. Madeline had coaxed some of Lena's story from her, and fixed on changing the girl's life around.

They went to bible classes, shopped for clothes and created fabulous vegetarian meals. When Lena was ready, Madeline had Lena born again and baptized. Because of her previous experience and wayward life, Lena's conversion was a star in the Baker's crown. Unfortunately, Lena just wanted to fit in. She did and said what others did and said. Lena didn't purposefully deceive God and the Baker family; she knew no other way to relate.

It was a beautiful fall weekend, the trees were turning oange, and the cool wind softened the affect of the sun. Madeline and George were napping in their room as Lena and Janet whispered quietly about nothing. It wasn't long before Janet drifted off into quiet slumber and Lena soon followed.

Janet was a pretty girl, with long straight copper colored hair and white skin. She could get second glances wherever she went. She wore no cosmetics, and plain boy clothes and a musky scent of leather. Clean sporty skin and nails. Light green eyes and thick full mouth. She was awkward with herself, and beautiful. She believed anything different was good. She liked Lena. Janet knew when she met Lena that she very different.

When Janet woke up that afternoon, the house was still quiet. She turned her head slightly to see the late sun streaming through the white gauze curtain of her bedroom. Next to her she looked at Lena sleeping. She looked like Snow White, she thought. Snow White with a golden tan, black hair, childlike slumber. She rose slowly from the bed and as quiet as possible shut the door, turning the knob so the latch wouldn't click. Slowly reaching up she slid the lock. Pausing, with her heart beginning to race, she listened to the slow steady breathing of the sleeping beauty lying on the bed. She looked at Lena's figure. She was wearing a campy gray dress her aunt had donated to the girl. Made of shiny cheap polyester, it buttoned up the front and had an elastic waste band. Lying on her side, with her arm under her pillow, the gray dress clung thinly to her figure. She wore no stockings; it was just to hot, and her bare feet looked a bit grungy on the white bedspread.

Janet walked quietly across the carpet and stood frozen beside it. With as little motion as possible, she resumed her position facing the sleeping girl. Janet was so close to Lena's face she imagined she could feel the girl's breath on her lips. The girl stirred. Frightened, Janet froze. Brown eyes began to appear and flutter, and lips parted slightly with a long exhale. Janet stared, not realizing she was holding her breath. Lena reached out her hand and stroked Janet's red mane, and then smiled. "Hi sleepy," Janet whispered.

It was more than Janet could take. Her heart pounded in her ears, making any communication inaudible.

The passion of youth guided their behavior. Just as Lena laid her hand on Janet's hair, Janet kissed Lena's mouth. That darling pouty bottom lip, the soft electricity of tongue, she put her arm around the girl, and drew her close. Janet felt a brief struggle, and held firm, until she felt the softness return.

They lay on their sides, facing each other, mouths locked in a confused kiss, until slowly Lena relaxed and Janet was sure it was okay to inch closer. Their bodies heating in the late afternoon sun.

Janet began to feel impatient. She straddled the girl's body, pelvis-to-pelvis, and relaxed on top of her. She leaned down and slowly kissed her neck and chest, unbuttoning her dress with one hand. When she couldn't unbutton any further, she placed a hard kiss on her mouth, and then got up. She removed her dress and bra; they lay together, arms and legs moving in lustful harmony, fingers and mouths searching for pleasure.

Twelve

Jack and Jill went up the hill, to fetch a pail of water.

Graduating from Spring Gulch Ranch was the first time Lena had completed anything beyond an orgasm. She showed up for dinner with a sense of pride. It was her day at last. But her party was uneventful. No one got in a fight, no one was sent away without dinner. No one threw food, and most noticeable, no one cried. No family attended.

Madeline Baker sat honorably at Lena's table, looking as if she were sitting in a leper colony. Shauna, Lena's closest friend, gave her a seashell hair clip. They all prayed over the mashed potatoes and fried chicken. Instead of going home after the party, like other graduating residents, Lena went to her small private room and sat on the end of her bed. Every thing was packed, and the walls looked ugly and gray.

It was the end of a very long year. Once again, change came in the spring for Lena. Tomorrow morning her case manager would arrive to take her back to Barberton, and her new foster family. She was neither excited nor nervous. She felt like she had lost all her reason to live, overwhelmed by the loss of a place she never allowed herself to value. She was once again leaving one place without knowing what the next might bring.

A nameless social worker picked her up and drove her to Barberton. They didn't talk during the seven-hour drive more then the polite short sentences necessary to take care of eating and using the rest room.

When they arrived it was evening. They drove up to the front of the house and parked the car. The house was old. It was a large two story with windows facing the west. Overgrown lilac bushes, shielding the lawn from the street and driveway, fenced in the yard. Inside the yard were cherry trees in full bloom. To Lena, it was like something out of a country living magazine.

The social worker got out and knocked on the door. A woman appeared. She was neither old nor young. But she was tired. She was small framed, with short, gray and brown hair. She wore a cross on a chain that hung down low.

"Hello Pete. I was expecting you. How was your trip?" Without waiting for an answer she turned to Lena, standing in the doorway. "Hi there. You must be Lena. My name is Miriam West, but you can call me mom, or Miriam. Frank will be here in a minute; he went out to the shop. He's working on the closet door for your room."

Lena was mute. Pete chatted about the trip, while carrying bags into the house and setting them in the front room.

The front room was large, as were all the rooms in the house, and looked as if it had been decorated in the 1960s. It had gold shag carpeting, bright gold and green lampshades, and a gold velvet couch. One entire wall was dedicated to family portraits of various sizes, most of them black and white. It looked and felt like a home.

When Pete was finished visiting, he gave Miriam his card and told her to call him if she needed anything. Then he got into his car and drove away.

"I'm sure everything will be just fine. Lena, would you like to get some of your things gathered up and I will show you to your room?"

Lena picked up her backpack and suitcase and followed Miriam through the kitchen, and up a steep set of stairs. At the top, they took a left and went into a large bedroom. She surveyed her surroundings. There was a twin bed with a quilt, a dresser and a nightstand, and a window with sheer curtains, facing west. The walls were flat white and undecorated. She set down her backpack on the bed, and her suitcase on the floor.

"The rules of the house are simple," Miriam began. "You keep your room and the bathroom up here clean. You must get up every morning on time for school. You must go to school. You must come home from school or have permission before you go anywhere other than here. You can use the phone only twice a day for no more than five minutes. You are allowed to go on a date Friday or Saturday only, and curfew time is 10:00 pm. For every five minutes you are late coming home from a date, you have to come in 15 minutes early the next time. You can spend the night or have a girlfriend over once a week if you are not on restriction. You will get restriction if you do not follow the rules.

"Dinner is at 5:30, and you must come to the table. You will be asked to help with dinner, or clean up after dinner, or both. We go to church every Sunday morning, and you are welcome to join us, but you do not have to. You are free to join another church, but you are responsible for your own transportation.

"If you need any items in the bathroom, I shop for them once a week, let me know ahead of time. If you need clothing, I can sew you some or request a voucher from Pete, and we can go shopping. If you want anything extra, I expect you to get a job. Chores are not paid. You do not get an allowance. I do the laundry once a week. You must have your laundry basket downstairs on laundry day, or you will have to wait another week.

"How does this sound?"

"Okay." Lena replied, although she was thinking that it sounded lengthy and complicated. And the woman's name confused her. Was it Marian, or Miriam? Did her name end with an N or an M?

"I might have missed a few things, but we can talk about them when, or if, they come up. Oh, Pete said you smoke. I don't approve of that, but I am not going to stop you. But there is no smoking upstairs, ever. Now, you can get settled in and unpack while I make dinner."

Going to school was not a choice open for debate in the foster home, and so Lena resigned herself to going. She was not humble about her reputation and experiences with her birth family in this small town; she was ignorant. She only knew that her mother had once again moved her brothers and sister to another community, and that somehow made her feel a little better.

Casey, short for Cassandra, was Lena's first and only girlfriend when she began school that fall. They met in gym class. Casey was taller than all her classmates. She had long golden brown hair with big green eyes. She had a natural beauty, with rose-colored cheeks, and an easy smile. She wore large rimmed glasses and was kind to everyone. Standing next to Lena, there couldn't have been two more opposite girls. That was the point.

Casey saw in Lena a brooding brunette with large brown eyes thickly lined in black cosmetics. She saw a girl with an uneasy temperament, always on the offense. Lena was considered new, even though she had attended briefly for a month before going to Spring Gulch, and it was rumored that she had been sent to the nut house. It was rumored she went insane and lived on the street as a prostitute. In a small town like Barberton, that was close to icon status for a teen.

The two girls had several classes together, and formed a spontaneous friendship. A month into the school year Casey was warned that if she hung around with Lena it would ruin her reputation. What that meant was, she wouldn't be in the A crowd, and wouldn't get invited to the good parties. She never shared this with Lena, but it was a hard decision. Lena wasn't the easiest person to be around. She lied frequently, making up stories that never happened. She didn't keep her word when she said she would do something. But Casey stayed the course and was committed to the friendship, good and bad.

Lena, on the other hand, did not have that kind of choice. She had one friend. Casey. Casey turned out to be a loyal, life-long friend. One of their favorite things to do was go to the pool Casey's parents owned. During the summer it was open to the public, but during the winter it was closed, and only used by the family. It made for great teen-age fun. At night when the snow was falling; they would get in the water and float on their backs, watching the snow drift down into the warm water. It was a magical place.

Friendship can change a person, and it did for Lena. She watched how her friend dressed and acted, trying to copy as much of her as possible. Casey became Lena's model for how to relate to teachers, her foster parents and other students. By watching Casey, Lena learned just enough about a normal daily life to respond with some accuracy to the stress of teenage living. She learned from Casey, who had her own problems with parents and schoolwork and life, that she wasn't alone in her desire to have a self-determined life. Casey wanted to be done with school and go out on her own. For teenagers, time seems to go very slow.

As pretty and aloof as a girl could possibly be, Lena had no dates for high school functions. She was sure she had a reputation of being fast and loose, even though she had dated no one. At school she avoided all connection or conversation with boys. Always slightly paranoid, she was suspicious of the boys. She was convinced all they wanted to do was 'kiss and tell.' If she was going to have a boyfriend, she decided, he would have to be out of school.

At a convenience store, while buying cigarettes, she met Kevin. Kevin had not finished school, and spent a great deal of time making up stories to get girls to go to bed with him. In 1984 terms, he was a 'happening dude.' Bulked up from building fences on a ranch, he didn't walk up to Lena; he swaggered. He used lines like "You aren't from around here, are you?" And, "Oh, really, I can't believe we've never met. I thought I had seen every beautiful woman in this dirty little town."

Lena bought it.

They dated several times. Then the relationship turned into having sex everyday. At lunch Kevin would pick Lena up at school in his little red Honda and they would go to his apartment above the closed butcher shop, and have sex. On the weekends they would party with his friends, Jerry and Frank. Sometimes Casey would join them. Casey despised Kevin from the start. She called him a jerk and a phony. But Jerry was okay, for a nerd, and Frank was kind of cute. When all five of them were together, they would drink and listen to music until 9:45, when Lena had to return to her foster home.

Kevin, a sociopath even at the age of twenty, was charming. He looked like Nicolas Cage, but with a chipped front tooth. He liked physical labor, but held no job. Kevin wanted to work in high-risk jobs, like car theft, armed robbery, or maybe the FBI.

He was casual about crime but extraordinarily serious about his health.

He worked out rigorously at the health club, posing in the mirror for himself. He bathed twice a day, although he had no job or place to be. He could tell you a story of robbing a store that you would swear on your mothers grave, had to be true. He told Lena that she was Bonnie, and he was Clyde. For Valentines Day, he bought Lena a white rabbit fur coat, and jumped out of a box painted like a cake, dancing like a male stripper.

When you have little or no boundaries, you learn from other's reactions, when you have crossed a social norm that is unacceptable. Kevin learned this way. Lena could be lovely and forgiving, but she was not without judgment. Kevin crossed the lines of decency many times, but it was when she found him in bed with his 13-year-old stepsister that she had to let him go. He had been fun, he had been useful, and he had been dangerous. Lena thought that it might have been love.

Lena sat at the breakfast counter at the foster home thinking about Kevin. He had begged and pleaded, and lied. Still she would not see him. It wasn't that she was angry. No, that would be easy. It is easy to be angry. She was sad. Lena knew Kevin was just being Kevin. He had no morals, which is what made him exciting. She just decided that she had to let him, and all his crazy energy, go. She sat at the breakfast counter with her face in her hands, when the phone rang.

It was Kevin. He said simply that he could never love anyone but her, and then he did the inexplicable. He fired a gun.

Lena let go of the phone and gasped for air. The group of adults sitting at the table next to her playing cribbage, looked up with alarm.

"What? What is it Lena?" Miriam was looking at Lena's shocked face. Lena's mouth was open, but no words were coming out.

Then Lena began to cry and mumble. Miriam called the police. Two hours later, Miriam got a call back saying that Kevin had not meant anything by it. He had been messing around, and a gun went off. He was Okay.

But Lena was not Okay. She went to bed and stayed there for a week. She just could not shake the feeling that something was terribly wrong with her. After dinner one night she went to her room and swallowed as many different pills as she could find. Sudafed, aspirin, Vivarin, cold medicine. Then she called Jerry and told him she was killing herself. Thanking him for the nice items and parties he had given her, she wanted him to know that life was just too confusing to go on. After they hung up, he called Mrs. West, who called her son over, and they all took her, kicking and screaming, to the emergency room, where the head nurse pumped her stomach. The Master from the local Heritage Christian Church was called to speak with Lena, who laid in the hospital bed feeling like an unspeakable failure.

"Why, Lena?" he asked, holding her hand. "You have all the reasons in the world to live."

"Live for what?" she questioned.

"For Jesus. For your future. For your foster parents." He continued to talk to her quietly about the God who understood her, but he had lost her attention. She stared out the hospital room window, deep in thought.

The hospital released her to go home, and the Master said he expected to see her in church on Sabbath. The incident added to Lena's internal data. Personal failure on public display is humiliating.

Thirteen

All around the mulberry bush, the monkey chased the weasel

Jerry was a lazy young man. Everyone knew it, including Jerry. He barely finished high school, only because his mother did most of his assignments. His parents, Ron and Martha, were devout Christians in the Heritage Christian Church. They worshipped on Saturday, ate only specially cleaned foods, and had strict rules to guide their every moment in life. They had rules on how to dress, speak, pray, eat, shop, work, and play. To put it simply, they had more rules on what not to do than the military. Jerry was the baby of the family, who still lived at home at age 21, and spent his days breaking all the rules and hiding the facts of his life. He had no job; his money came from his parents, who assisted him with an allowance of $100 a week. With that money he smothered Lena with gifts.

At school Lena received gifts of flowers and stuffed animals, perfume, scarves. She would hear her name over the intercom system. She needed to come to the office, and she would return to the classroom with some item that indicated she had an admirer. On the weekends he would pick her up for church, and they would go for donuts and coffee, a sin in the eyes of the church. Jerry's attention impressed her far more than his person, and he knew it. He didn't care. He was crazy about her. She was fun and exciting, like no other girl he had ever met. She had that brooding dark secrecy about her that fascinated him. When she drank, she was funny and loose and carefree. When she was sober, she was sullen and unhappy. Above all, he wanted to make her happy.

Lena was in her foster home a year before she went to see her birth family. Elizabeth had moved to Lafarge when Lena was at Spring Gulch Ranch. Lafarge was a windy little town the same size as Barberton, 50 miles to the north. During a Family Service visit at the West's foster home, Pete mentioned that Lena might consider going to visit her mother, sister and brothers. Curious, she asked for their phone number. He didn't have the number, he said, but he knew her mother was working at Lenny's Restaurant and Bar.

The next weekend Jerry drove her to Lafarge. It was early afternoon when they parked at the restaurant. They went inside and waited to be seated. A familiar looking woman approached them with menus.

"Hi there. Welcome to Lenny's. Smoking or non-smoking?"

"Mom, its me," Lena offered.

"Punk? Punk! Well hello there!" Elizabeth embraced her oldest daughter warmly. Lena felt stiff, like plastic.

"How are you?" Elizabeth asked.

"Okay. This is Jerry. He drove me here."

"Nice to meet you Jerry. Glad to see my daughter has a chauffeur. Oh, uh, let me introduce you to Gene." They followed Elizabeth to the coffee counter where a middle-aged man sat sipping coffee.

"Gene this is Punk, my oldest daughter." The expression on his face was nothing less then complete astonishment. Then he looked bewildered. "Well, Elizabeth, you told me you had six children, but I only counted five. I just assumed the sixth was dead or something."

The group went silent momentarily. Then Lena said, "No, I'm alive...still. And my name is Lena."

"Punk is her nickname. I guess she's outgrown it. Hey, you guys gonna stay for a while? I gotta get on with my shift. Why don't you visit with Gene, and I'll check back in a little bit?"

They moved to a booth and slid in. It was one of those half circle booths, and she was in the middle. She sat there thinking how she just wanted to get out, but was trapped between two men she could care less about.

Elizabeth brought them coffee. That was weird.

"So," Gene began, "you're the sixth one. Wow! I never asked about you because I thought something terrible had happened to you, that you died...and that's why no one mentioned you."

"Technically, I am the third child. Are you and mom dating or something?"

"Oh, didn't she tell you? We got married right after Christmas."

"Well, that's great. Congratulations. Do you think it would be okay to go and see my sister?"

"Oh sure. Let me tell you how to get there." He proceeded to take a pen out of his pocket and write on a napkin the address with a little street map.

Elizabeth came by to refill the coffee, and sat down. "So did you tell them the big news?" She didn't wait for a reply. "Isn't he just wonderful?" It wasn't really a question. Elizabeth put her arm around Gene and gave him a squeeze.

"Uh...Lena here was saying that she wanted to go up to the house and see her sister and brother."

"Well, I really don't think you should right now. Jean is with her girlfriend horseback riding and Tony is not supposed to let anyone in the house when we're not home."

"Where is everyone else?"

"Oh, well," she let out a sigh. "Harlan is with his father in Arizona. Web got married to a girl here in town and they live in their own place. Lee got this girl pregnant, and so he dropped out of school to work and take care of her and the new baby. Jean and Tony are the only ones at home right now."

"And that's the way it's gonna stay," Gene said in a slow, low, and most manly voice.

There was a momentary silence, in which Lena had time to digest the information she had just received. Then she was done with the scene.

"Well, it was nice seeing you again." She shoved Jerry to get him to move so she could get up. He was in no hurry, so she shoved him again.

"Hey, what's the rush? You just got here; can't you stay a little while?" Elizabeth sounded amused.

"Oh, I have to get back. I got some chores and stuff to do. You know." Lena was standing, putting on her jacket.

Elizabeth stood up and hugged her daughter. "I'll get the coffee for you," she said.

"Thanks. Bye. Nice meeting you Gene. Bye."

When they were back in the car, Jerry asked, "Why did we leave so soon? She wanted to visit."

"Why?" He really is a bit slow, Lena thought.

"Why what?" Jerry questioned.

"Why should I have stayed and visited?"

"Because she is your mom and you haven't seen her in two years. Haven't you missed her?"

"Miss her. What is there to miss? She never cared. Is that so hard to believe?"

"Then why did we come here?"

"I just wanted to see if I would feel any different. I don't."

"Different than what?"

"I wanted to see if some good memory would come back to me. My counselor at Spring Gulch said that the bad memories fade away, and someday I will be able to remember the good times and feelings. She thought for a moment. Maybe there aren't any. Besides, now we have time to party."

"Okay." That ended the topic on an upbeat note.

They drove down the freeway listening to "Huey Lewis and the News" sing about love.

Fourteen

This little froggy took a big leap,
This little froggy took a small,

Graduating from the fringe meant getting married. In 1985, when Lena was 18, and students her age were leaving high school and Barberton for some unplanned adventure in college or a big city, Lena took her GED test, and put the final details together for her wedding. It was the natural outcome of the path she was on. She simply bought the ticket and took the ride. It is not unusual for young people who have lost, or never had, the American Dream Family, to want it. And it is not unusual for young people to create that family as soon as they are able. Lena believed she could have a normal life once she was an adult. No more foster home, no more educational dictates, a real life awaited her. This was the big IT for Lena.

Marriage and family were the big exit door from childhood to adulthood, and more important, from the fringe to a real life. It meant she would have a family, a purpose, and a position within society. All her hopes and dreams, her identity, were waiting for her within the sanctity of marriage. She sat in her room daydreaming of her own home, finally having control of her own destiny, and (of course) love would finally be hers. Getting married meant she had acquired love. Acquired love, not fallen into, not given, but obtained that elusive joy through forcible entry and theft. Her past, and all the compost that came with it, Lena believed, would be left behind.

It was sad really, that Jerry did not receive guidance in the fantasy he was manufacturing for Lena. If he had, he may never have proposed.

It wasn't as though he didn't have people who cared about him. They just didn't speak out. He had an older brother and sister, parents, church masters. All were mute.

Not one individual in the small community asked him what he was doing sleeping with and supplying alcohol to a teenager. It was obvious to everyone that knew him, after her suicide attempt, that she was not stable enough to make a life-long decision. Not one person had enough insight to suggest to the smitten, but foolish, young man that marrying such a girl might turn out badly for him later. After all, girls occasionally learn who they are, and leave for a life that they should have waited for.

Engagements and weddings are funny, but not in the ha-ha sort of way. They are culturally and symbolically cruel. Lena and Jerry's was no different. It was a six-month engagement. Of course he proposed on Valentine's Day, and did it with much glamour and fan fair. There were the dozen red roses, the candy and the rings. It was just like in a cheesy romance novel or an afternoon movie. Everyone knew about it ahead of time. All peripheral people were thrilled at the perfect union of the sweet couple formed out of poverty and boredom in a small town. A delusional happiness everyone wanted to believe in.

The wedding itself was simple. Miriam made the dresses for Lena and Casey, who agreed to be the maid of honor. Lena spent all her savings from her job at the mini mart on flowers and cake and invitations. She invited everyone she despised. She wanted to use the significant event to show her birth family that she was indeed a worthy human being, and loved by many. Then, she thought, they would feel bad for having treated her so badly. She didn't know how desperately immature that was, or she may have realized she was too young to agree to a lifelong relationship. But, of course, she couldn't know what she didn't know.

Three days before the wedding, a stranger in a bookstore gave her some truth. Lena and Casey were wasting the morning hours browsing the bookshelves for a journal to transcribe the details of their summer into. A woman approached Lena, looking nervous, she said, "You're Lena, aren't you?"

"Yeaaaa." She said slowly.

"You are getting married to Jerry this weekend…"

"Yea…."

"Don't do it," the woman blurted forcefully. It was odd sounding, as if she were being forced to say it.

"Excuse me?"

"Don't marry him. Please. I've known him and his family all my life. We raised our families together. He's a nice boy. But, you see…oh dear. He is not right for you. He will never be strong enough for you."

Not quite sure she was hearing correctly, Lena repeated what had been said. "You are a friend of his parents, and you are telling me that I shouldn't marry him…. Maybe you should be talking to him… Or his mom."

"I know I am out of place with this. I have talked to Martha. All she can see is how happy her son is. She loves you, and she wants you both to be happy, but it won't last. He is wrong for you".

Lena looked around and saw that the store clerk and a customer had stopped talking, and were looking their way. She walked further down the isle of books leaving Casey at the journal section, hoping to either get away from the woman, or at least keep the conversation private.

Lena pretended to be interested in a book on dolphins. She stared at the cover and said with quiet disbelief, "Don't you think I know who is right for me? What do you mean, he will never be strong enough? I've never met you, how do you know what I want?"

"What do you want? A family? Children? Love?"

Lena nodded, still looking at the book in her hand.

The woman softened her voice, almost to a whisper. "He is a nice guy. He is faithful to the church. He loves his mother. He loves you... but he is not capable of caring for himself. As soon as you marry him, he will expect you to take care of him." She paused. With a sadness that would have convinced the most stubborn person, she said, "He will never be able to give you what you need from a man."

Lena reacted with the only thing she knew. Defense. She replied, "Well, aren't you the best friend a family could ever have, three days before their son's wedding you try and ruin it? Don't you think it is a bit late for this kind of chat?"

"You are right. It is the eleventh hour. But my loyalty isn't to Jerry or his mother, it is to women. We are both women. Do you think your dreams are any different than mine, or my sisters, or my daughters? You deserve to know the truth, as a woman."

They stood in silence, looking at the bookshelf, feeling the summer heat. Suddenly feeling tired of the conversation; she asked the unavoidable question that had to be asked in order to end the unfortunate meeting. Lena looked into the woman's face, tightened her jaw and said with barely hidden anger, "what truth would that be?"

"He is a simple young man. At 23, he has never had a job, and still lives with his mother. She does his laundry and cooks and cleans for him. You are a complicated... dynamic young woman. Your search is for yourself. He will become an anchor around your neck."

Lena let out a sigh of relief. "I don't think so. He will grow and change. It is past time that he gets a life of his own. Thank you for your concern, but I really do think a person can change and grow from experience.... He really does need some experience outside of this small town. Once we are away from his parents, he will become more..." She didn't finish her sentence, because she couldn't find the word.

"Please don't be angry with me. As a woman, I had to tell you what's in my heart. Please, please, just postpone the wedding. It's not too late. Really. It's not too late."

"I will think about what you said. Thank you for your concern." Lena turned, leaving the woman standing in the isle, and walked outside, still holding the book. She walked back in, sat it on the counter, and without explanation, walked back out into the hot July sun.

Casey joined Lena as she walked and lit a Marlboro.

"Hey, what was that about? It looked private, so I didn't interrupt. Who was that? Why did you just leave me in there?"

"Some friend of Jerry's family. She wanted to talk to me about the wedding."

"Oh. Well, what's wrong? What'd she say to you?"

"Nothing."

"Talk to me, Lena. I hate it when you are like this. Tell me what she said."

"It's nothing, really. Come on, let's go." They got into the red Honda Civic she had borrowed from Jerry.

Lena took Casey home, and then went back to Miriam's. The first thing she did was call Jerry.

"Hi. What's up?"

"Hey, I need to talk to you. Can you come over later?" Lena asked.

"Yea. What's up?"

"Nothing, I just need to talk to you, that's all."

"Okay. What time?"

"Is seven okay?"

"Sure, see you then. I love you."

"I love you too." Lena hung up the phone and went outside. It was a beautiful summer day.

Lena was sitting on the front porch at seven thirty five, when Jerry drove up. She had been thinking, and rehearsing different ways to say what she was going to say, for three hours. Still, she did not know how to get it out. They walked to the park across the street, and sat on the swings.

"What's wrong? I'm getting the feeling you are upset about something."

"I need to talk to you."

"Okay. I'm listening."

They were quiet for a while, and then Lena began. "I am wondering if we should put off the wedding for a while. I'm having second thoughts. Maybe we should just live together."

"I told you. It's against everything my church and family believe in. We can't be together if we don't get married. Are you saying you don't want to marry me, three days before the wedding? This is classic. This happens all the time. People get cold feet all the time. But it isn't reality. What is reality is that we are getting married on Sunday."

"Well, I…I am feeling unsure now. I am beginning to wonder if we are rushing into it."

"No, we are not. Listen to me; we've been together for two years. You are just tired and stressed out. We are not calling this off. You have family coming in from Alaska and Arizona. I have family coming in from the East Coast. We are not calling this off because you are having feelings."

She could have reminded the boy who had nothing to loose, that she was the one paying for the wedding, not him. She could have admitted she did not have feelings for him, but only desired a family. She should have told him she didn't care if it hurt his pride to be ditched three days before the end of her life as an individual… but she didn't.

She looked at him. He was right. She could rely on his common sense any day of the week. She wanted to believe in their dreams, in the Heritage Church. She wanted to believe something good was happening in her life.

"Yeah. Okay. You're right. Hey, now that I am eighteen, I have until 11; let's get some rum and coke and go over to Ron's house. His parents are gone, and Casey said she was going to bake special brownies and watch some scary movie on HBO."

"Yeah. Sounds good." He looked at her suspiciously; wondering if winning an argument with her was really that easy.

They walked back to the house, got into the Jerry's white 1973 Mustang and drove to the liquor store.

On the day of the wedding, everyone arrived at the West's because it was too early to arrive at the city park, where the ceremony was to be held. Unable to emotionally deal with her birth family, Lena refused to come downstairs to greet them. Miriam, to the best of her ability, tried to visit with Elizabeth, but was unsuccessful. Her house was unexpectedly full of people neither of the West's knew, or cared to know. When Jimmy arrived with his wife Jane, Elizabeth went out and sat in the car. Eventually, everyone left to get lunch and meet at the city park, the ceremony site.

There were only two people Lena wanted to see. Her sister Jean, a bridesmaid, and Casey, her maid of honor. Jean and Casey had arrived early the evening before, and spent the entire night visiting with Lena. Around five that morning, they slept briefly, then woke exhausted. Casey and Jean both tried to keep the conversation casual that morning. They had both experienced Lena running away from life, and didn't want to have to report to the family that they didn't know where the bride was. But the bride did not run away.

Fifteen

Fiddle dee dee, Fiddle dee dee, the fly married the bumble bee

Lena and Jerry's life was incredibly normal. It followed that predictable, semi-successful pattern young families adhere to. Seven years of events can be summed up in this design.

First: Move away from the parents. Their new life began in a much larger town. They moved right after the wedding to a town in Southern Oregon, where it never snowed, and the flowers were always in bloom. It was a magical place, in a magical time of their lives. Their great and fresh illusion began with a change of environment that did not include any childhood reminders.

Second: Establish a network of married people who have the kind of life you want. It so happened that the Heritage Church in the town of Riverdale, Oregon was expecting the newlyweds, and within six months, had helped them put together a reasonably comfortable life. Jerry began working as a carpet installer for a member of the church, and Lena taught a free morning exercise class, open to members. They purchased a small home across the river, and became regular members of the congregation. It was all quite easy.

Third: Have several children that you spend all your time and resources nurturing. From the moment of conception Lena was devoted to the care and well being of both her daughters.

Not only did they give her life meaningful experience, but she also learned the lesson of selfless servitude necessary to be a parent. Later in life, Lena would succumb to an education, and learn in a social economics class the ugly, hidden truth: children are non-contributing liabilities.

The completion of these three tasks is made possible by the married couples' ability to conform to the cultural environment and convert to the spiritual principles of the moral majority. These two key elements, conforming to the culture and following the moral majority, are so powerful that the American Family is almost exclusively born under these conditions.

For Lena, who was trying to escape the fringe, it is not unreasonable to want to blend into the fabric, and there is no better place to do this than in church. The Heritage Christian Church exists to pull the raw dough from the main dish, roll it out flat, add a few sprinkles of holiness, and cut precisely the correct shape of character that God intended his humans to have. The leftover pieces are what they call sin, which, if not disposed of properly, will rot.

That was the mistake Lena made. She did not properly dispose of her leftovers, and they became rotten, stinking up her life, and the atmosphere of the family around her. But I am getting ahead of the story. First comes the family.

The Heritage Christian Church is the same as any other religion. It has a specific purpose: To caste the evil from the lives of its members, protect members from evildoers, and guide members to correct the flaws in their lives. For those unfortunates, such as Lena, who are discovered to have faulty beginnings, the Heritage Church uses them to symbolize the conversion process. It is important with indoctrination that examples are made of those who are righteous and those who are damned. In the

7 years that Jerry, Lena and their babies attended the Heritage Church, Lena would symbolize both.

It wasn't a spiritual quest, but practicality that made the church a good place to go. On Sabbath, the Church was filled with goodwill and kindness. During the weekdays, it provided free food, clothes, exercise classes, and soul-searching studies of the Bible. They had to be loyal to the Church; Jerry found a job there. For six years the family stayed close to the center of the pew, so to speak. They neither questioned nor confessed. It was the happiest time for Jerry and Lena. Most of all, Lena didn't ever have to think about where she came from.

Lena chose to forget the first fifteen years of her life. Oh, she knew what her name was, who her parents were, and the names of her siblings. But she couldn't tell you who her friends were or what they did for fun during those years. She couldn't tell you what her favorite Christmas or birthday memory was. She especially couldn't tell you what she was doing when she was fifteen. Those memories were gone; displaced like a trivial item such as a pen or comb. But deep in her denial sat a restlessness that confused her. The kind of knowing something was wrong, but not knowing what is was, that made her nervous. Like sands through the hour-glass of the soap opera she watched, Lena's life slowly, dramatically, moved forward.

During the seventh year of their residency in Riverdale, Lena was discovered having an affair with an outsider, an affair with a non-churchgoing individual. It was by accident that on a night of drinking and sexual exploitation, a police officer responded to a call at a home where the individual needed assistance to remove handcuffs from his partner. This individual's name was Ryan and his partner in need of assistance, was Lena. The responding officer was a well-liked individual from church, who freed Lena from bondage, and took her to the emergency room for a sprained wrist.

The circumstances got worse when she admitted to having additional affair with a school board member. The situation was humiliating, as Lena was a Sabbath School teacher, and child-care provider for many of the church members. And so it was that the girl who had been rescued from the edge of poverty and self-destruction was banished to the side of the evildoers. Lena knew of only one thing to do in such a situation. Move and start over. And so they packed their family, sold the house and moved to a pretty community in the center of the great state of Oregon.

Moving wasn't a bad idea. They had been kids when they moved to Riverdale. Besides, they needed a bigger community, one with a university and more economic opportunities. Jerry found a new job, and Lena found a better house than they had in Riverdale. She recommitted herself to being a good parent and wife, doing the things good mothers and wives do. For Lena, this lasted another five years. In the end though, it was boredom, alcoholism and untreated emotional wounds that overtook the monotonous, passionless and apathetic life Lena had embraced for 12 years.

Sixteen

Old Mother Hubbard went to the cupboard

Have you ever gotten the feeling that you are not using as much of your mind as you could be? You play along as if your life is your idea, but you know that you are doing what you're supposed to do because you don't know anything else. It is that realization: the idea that she might be following a path designed by someone else, that made Lena begin to question her life.

Jerry and Lena had lived in Central Oregon for over a year, when Lena came to the realization that her drinking was affecting how she managed, or rather, didn't manage, her life. Living in a trailer park, destitute from living on Jerry's small salary, and spending her days with two small children, Lena questioned why she drank so much, why she couldn't seem to be faithful to Jerry, and why she wanted desperately to leave the planet. Lena believed that if she knew why, she would find the key to success and happiness. For the next four years, this is what she did.

"Take a good look in the mirror," Ellen answered one January afternoon. Faith was napping, and Dawn was still at school. It was a cold day, temperature in the 20's. The interior of the home was isolated from the bright blue sky and snow-covered ground by heavy drapes. Dim artificial light softened the green shag carpet and dark wall paneling.

Lena went to the oval mirror in the living room. "What do you see? Lena asked. Without waiting for an answer, she continued. "I will tell you what you see. You are fat. You are lazy. Look around. You don't care what kind of housewife you are."

Lena sighed and went into the kitchen. She got out the crockpot and filled it half full of water. Then she added some stew meat and salt. She turned the pot onto med and placed the lid over it. Still thinking about what Ellen said she went back to the mirror.

"If I am unhappy because I am fat, all I have to do is lose the fat! How hard can that be? Really Ellen! You talk as if I were terminally this way. I can change." With this she walked back into the kitchen and made herself a cup of tea and brandy. "I am feeling better about myself already," Lena said.

"Really? It is that easy?" Ellen responded with amusement. "Well, let me show you what you refuse to see. Go look in the mirror again. Look real hard. You will see your father's eyes staring back at you. That is what you will see. As long as you live, you will be wearing his eyes. It was his only gift, a permanent souvenir from your childhood. Those large dark brown windows which look out at the world."

"You know Ellen," Lena said calmly, "I don't have to listen to you." She got up and fixed herself another tea and brandy.

That evening at dinner the family of four sat looking at the stew and corn bread Lena had fixed. Dawn had just turned seven and sat on her knee's to avoid using a booster seat. Faith sat next to Lena in the booster seat, so Lena could cut up her meat for her.

"I don't want this momma", Dawn whined, and wrinkled her nose. She looked down at her plate of meat and vegetables in brown sauce. "It don't look good."

"But it is good hunny. Just try it. See momma." Lena took a bite. "Mmm, good potatoes. Mmm, good carrots." She said, smiling at Dawn's scowling face.

"Why do you have to over salt everything? That's why she won't eat it." Jerry said.

Lena looked at Faith and then over at Dawn, who sat without speaking. "Okay hunny, what do you want?"

"Peanut butter and jelly!" she yelled enthusiastically.

"How 'bout you baby? You want a peanut butter and jelly sandwich?" Dawn nodded. "Momma fix you a sandwich." Lena got up and took the girls plates. She went into the kitchen and began fixing their sandwiches.

"Would you bring me another beer when you're done?" Jerry yelled.

"Sure." Lena brought the beer and sandwiches she had cut into four squares back into the dining room. She set the plates down. "What do you say?" she asked Dawn.

"Thank you Momma," Dawn said as she began eating.

Lena sat down. "I saw the funniest commercial today, Jer."

"Really."

"Yea. It was for colored contacts. Contact lenses for people who don't need glasses, they just want to change their eye color."

Jerry looked up from his bowl of stew. "Who would want to do that? Hey, did you call Shawna today? Are we going to get together this weekend?"

"Oh, yea. She's coming over later." Lena sat down and began trying to convince Faith to take a bite of her stew, but she would have none of it.

That day began a series of attempts made by Lena to change what she was. In her naive way, she simply wanted to become okay. If she were okay, she would not need to drink. If she didn't need to drink, she wouldn't. If she didn't drink, she would find freedom.

For two years Lena used every method she could imagine to change her life. The first thing Lena tried to do was change her appearance. This involved a series of bazaar choices. To an outsider, not knowing what she was trying to accomplish, the girl with the purples eyes, short black hair wearing an ill fitted black suit and tie with tennis shoes, shepherding two young girls through the sale rack at Goodwill, was a peculiar sight. If you were close enough to smell her however, you would understand. She was continuously intoxicated.

The next method was to move. Jerry sold property he had inherited from his aunt as a child, and used the money for a down payment on a beautiful new home, in a beautiful new neighborhood. Both girls began going to school a few blocks away, and Lena spent her days decorating and cleaning, and then redecorating each room. Every room, every season, got a new color of paint. She measured each new project by how much alcohol it took to complete it. Painting the bathroom was a six-pack of

Henry's. Painting the living room was a half case. Looking for a Christmas tree was a pint of scotch. A parent-teacher conference was a bottle of wine.

After the newness of the house wore off, Lena decided she would only drink at home, which worked out pretty well. Unfortunately, the cost of the new house became overwhelming to Jerry, and Lena decided that the way to not drink so much was to work while the kids were in school.

Alcoholics try many different methods to get their problem under control. Lena was no exception. She switched from wine to beer, gaining 60 additional pounds to her already overweight body. She agreed to stop drinking if she ever got fired from her job. In 1996 she had fourteen jobs, and began binge drinking on the weekends. She promised herself she would only drink during special events, and then nearly every day found a reason to host a special event, with lots of people and a party.

She joined a health club, had another affair, and switched from beer to scotch. She went to a therapist, went to church, got another job, went back to school, quit school, volunteered at girl scouts, got her real estate sales license. Nothing worked. She drank because she had to drink. She was at the end of her resources. She could not think of anything else to do. She hated who she was drunk, and she hated who she was sober. Two years of self-guided attempts at sobriety had produced no results, and it was at that point she became willing to listen to suggestions from someone who had successfully accomplished sobriety.

In 1997 Lena began attending AA meetings. Every day for nine months she went to meetings and cried. She cried the most self- indulgent tears ever delivered. By the end of her first year sober, she actually got tired of her own self-pity. To Lena, self-pity didn't matter. What mattered was that she was sober. Unhappy, but sober, Lena began waiting for a miracle.

Seventeen

There was a crooked man, who walked a crooked mile

Fringe people often live in self-imposed intellectual and emotional cages in order to secure themselves from themselves. This is the case with Lena. She knows that her natural boundaries are outside those of the rest of society, she knows the consequences of nonconformity, so she cages her desires in order to restrain them from overtaking her life. But freedom is a primal instinct, and will find a way to liberate itself. It found the perfect opportunity one day at the supermarket ATM.

Lena was curious at seeing an ATM with its front panel open and its money cartridges out in the main corridor of the busy supermarket. A man was crouched in front of the machine with his head nearly inside. His tool bag was open and exposed next to him.

"Hi," said Lena.

"The machine is down. I am not sure when it will be back up. There is another machine in the parking lot kiosk," he said without removing his head from the inside of the machine. His voice sounded as if it were passing through a tunnel.

"Really? I don't need a receipt." She was trying to be funny. It never worked, and today was no exception.

Pissed off by the intrusion, he pulled his head out of the ATM and turned around to find a surprising face. The boiling impatience he had been feeling evaporated.

"Oh, hi. I was…trying to be funny. I'm sorry." Embarrassment came up in Lena's face, and she looked at the tiled floor. She knew this man from her voyage into Alcoholics Anonymous meetings.

"Hi. It's you. Yeah, okay, how much you need? Twenties okay? I don't need this job. As a matter of fact, I hate this job. The only reason I keep it is the chance of suffering a fatal heart attack during a robbery. That'd put me out of my miserable, pathetic life."

And so began a friendship.

Experienced in the fringe, Michael saw the gauze Lena had wrapped tightly around herself. Maybe it was amusement, maybe it was pity, but he took every opportunity he could to unravel her.

Lena had been sober for a year when she began her friendship with Michael. She had every reason not to like him. He was a white male with a hot temper and a loud mouth. He was egocentric and 20 years her senior. He made odd personal references to alcohol and drug addiction, in front of other people. Lena was embarrassed by his freedom of dialog.

He was also the epitome of the good old boy system. He had two years of college and made three times as much as his female counterpart. He believed wives were something you attain, and children were non-contributing liabilities, to be seen and not heard.

Michael was disillusioned by the contribution his generation had made to the culture, to society. He was from Chicago, went to Vietnam, and had 16 years in recovery from drug addiction. A computer engineer who worked from his home and on the road, he had a fatalist view of reality.

He had no children, claimed to have raised two wives, but confessed he did a poor job of it. Both women left angry and resentful of his demanding nature and insatiable sexual play. After his second divorce he told Lena he was done with marriage. He said that women were "just too much fucking work." Closer to the truth was that he felt the relationships cost too much and delivered too small of a return.

But Michael had one thing that charmed Lena, real stories of life and love, grotesque failure and recovery from addiction. And when his commentary failed to bring her out of her shell, he amused her with colorful metaphors of the common transactions in life. Over endless cups of coffee and 12-step meetings, she learned to value a man as a person.

The conversations began at Lena's request. He wasn't always nice. But he spoke in a exposed, crazy way. She had no idea how a man could speak with so much tastelessness, not caring what others might think of him.

They mostly met in coffee shops. They had the kind of conversations that people eaves-drop on. It wasn't intentional. You could no more keep from staring at a naked woman walking down the street then they could keep from listening to their words.

"Tell me about men," she'd start.

"Get naked, bring beer," was his instant reply.

"Is it really that simple?"

"You would know, you've been married for 12 years. If given the choice, would Jerry make that request?"

"Yeah, sad to say. I despise that, you know? That boorish simplicity."

"So you are in a long term-relationship with an individual you really don't like. How predictable. Women do that. They marry a man, and then tell him how to change. Tell me about women."

Lena thought for a moment. "I think men want a woman with a pretty face, because it makes it easier for them to share power. If you want to have a good relationship with a man, if I want to have a good relationship with a man, I must constantly watch my look good in order for him to want me, therefore want to share power with me. If I want to have some say over something of value, it is easier if I have my look good on. It's like a guy can sooth his wounded super ego by saying 'at least she's pretty', or 'at least she gives me some'. Its sad to say, but I don't believe in the marriage institution honestly represents itself. It is really about men pretending they want the participation of a woman in their life, but in fact, it's all about the fuck."

"Michael replied, I think God made man because he was disappointed with monkeys, but the men didn't turn out much better. If I were a woman, I'd be a lesbian. Women are far more capable of evolving."

"I don't know about that. I just get frustrated, that's all. It's like men's expectations from woman are so ridiculously shallow and low, and women don't rise above it. So what happened to your marriages?"

"I wanted to create a life of my own design. My first marriage doesn't count, because I was so loaded all the time, I didn't recognize any motivation or intentions outside of getting loaded. In my second marriage, I went with the thought, 'My first marriage was so bad, I'll do the opposite.' The problem was, she never really liked who I was, not suave enough... and too crude."

They went to coffee regularly for a year at the coffee shop on the corner. They watched the tree foliage turn in the fall, drop its leaves, and be laid to rest, covered with a blanket of snow. They watched the spring sunshine come and gently wake up the hibernating life, and begin the growing process. Then one February day, Lena needed help. The kind of help only damaged people can offer damaged people. She let him in on her secret. She told him she was insane. There they were, the world crazily moving around them, when they met each other spiritually.

Eighteen

I do not like the Doctor Fell, the reason why I cannot tell.

Two years had passed since Lena had taken her last drink. She was close to finishing her bachelor's degree in economics. She had lost 60 pounds and had 'set a higher standard' for herself and family. That meant she had organized her responsibilities and met them with strict standards.

It was January. Her sister Jean and husband Steve came to live in their community. Lena had been writing Jean, begging her to move for several years, and the time had finally arrived. Jean and her family had been living in New Mexico, where the industry was so poor, they decided to try someplace new.

For Jean, that first year in rural Central Oregon would be the most traumatic time of her life. She had managed to separate her childhood from her future, and had a lovely family, with a bit of happiness. But being near her sister, after all the years that had passed, sent her on a roller coaster of power struggles and apologies. It was exhausting.

It was the same for Lena. Sobriety had helped her achieve major goals in her life. It also created a mean and demanding woman who walked over anyone who didn't agree with her view of a strict and unrelenting societal standard. After 12 years of binge drinking, extra marital affairs and what some might call neurotic behavior, Lena swung the opposite direction to become a bitchy, uptight, demanding (but sober) Mother.

On the second Thursday in February Lena knew the Jean's eight-month-old baby was sick. He ate very little, he was hot, and he coughed a lot. She had to say something, regardless of the power struggle that had developed between Jean and herself. As adults, Lena and Jean had two differing opinions about their childhood experience. Lena held her Mother and Father liable for the poverty and cultural illiteracy that she and her siblings had endured. Jean believed Lena's distain for her family was a result of Lena's need to prove she was better then the rest of the family.

Now those childish roles spelled disaster for the baby boy they both adored. Lena, in her most persuasive manipulative way could not get Jean to take the child to the doctor. Jean, attempting to prove her parental knowledge and skill, resented being told what to do by her know-it-all, 'educated' sister.

Five days later the baby was rushed to the hospital. Lena stood outside ICU, and with emotional daggers, sliced her sister to shreds. She accused Jean of putting her own ego above the health of her child. She accused her of stupidity and ignorance. And when Jean cried, Lena righteously forgave her with soothing words, rage still alive in her face and heart. Unable to stand the torment, Jean went home. Lena stayed at the hospital on day two and three, going home only for a late night nap and early morning shower.

Rage is not static. Unstable, it is in a constant state of change. Lena's rage grew. But she had plenty of help. Her small circle of friends were well acquainted with what she called "the standard," the excuse she used to practice intolerance toward those who did not manage life in the correct manner. They were appalled at the tragedy, and gave Lena support for her selfless act of child protection. After all, this was one of the reasons she chose the friends she did.

By day 10, the baby boy had endured surgery to remove fluid from his lungs. He was finally out of ICU, and in his own room on the fourth floor. Lena looked at this little body, only eight months old. A beautiful baby with blond hair and fair skin. He didn't even make a sound when he cried. The tears slid quietly down his cheeks into his ears. Not a sound was made as he lay with the respirator on, tied in restraints with the needles in his arms and a monitor hooked to his foot.

The days had turned into a nightmare for both women. When Lena looked at the baby, she felt rage toward Jean. But when she looked in the mirror, she felt rage toward herself for being who she was.

The days pass slowly for families in the hospital. For Jean, hope and faith were gifts from God. But nothing of a spiritual nature could have penetrated Lena's rage. The best she could give her sister was condescending sympathy.

Lena began to look for a way out of the intensity of her emotions. The days had consisted of getting to the hospital by 6 a.m. for the shift change and the night nurses' report, running home to take her own two children to school, and then going back to the hospital. In the afternoons she would pick up the girls from their small private Christian school outside of town and take them home before going back to the hospital. Jerry would bring the girls to the hospital for dinner. Once the baby was asleep for the night, she would go home. After 10 days, what little emotional strength she had stockpiled for just such an emergency, was used up. Bitterness filled her whole being.

On day 10 the baby went to X-ray early in the afternoon. The doctor wanted to see if there was still fluid on his lungs, and if so, where it was. The baby was still not able to breathe fully on his own. Everyone was concerned. Lena walked down the long corridor in the basement of the hospital. She hadn't been in this part of the hospital. The corridors were silent. Turning a corner she came upon a nurse's station. A male and two female nurses were talking and laughing. She asked for X-ray. They directed Lena to turn right and down one door, but to wait outside the room. She obeyed and sat on the floor outside the room by the door marked X-ray. An hour slid by. No one went in or out of the room.

Lena went back to the nurse's station. "How long will it take?" She inquired. The same nurse from earlier couldn't say, as they only did scheduling and assistance. Lena could feel herself become impatient with their obvious incompetence. She curtly told them she would be back in an hour, then turned to walk down the corridor. As she made her way to the elevator, Lena heard them discuss the child, "Poor baby. They shouldn't allow some people to have children." As she continued to walk, something inside her snapped.

Lena's head began to run away. "Medication. That's what I need. Everyone in this fucking hospital is medicated but me." She waited at the elevator, and rode it to the first floor. With her head down, she walked out the front doors. "It is so fucking cold today," she says out loud. It was the end of February, and the air felt thin and clear. The sun is too bright for her eyes. She got into her station wagon. As she drove out of the hospital parking lot, she dialed Michael on the cell phone. Lena knew she was in trouble.

It was Tuesday morning, and Michael was out of town. He felt distant on the phone. She hung up. Lena's mind began to tumble into a black hole, losing touch with the real world.

"Medication. That's what I need. Not love. Not understanding. Not recovery. What has it gotten me? A life full of shit. Shit from the past, shit now. No future. Two years without a drink, and this is what I get?"

And so, Lena drove to the liquor store and bought a fifth of Black Velvet and a Diet Coke from the cooler. The clerk asked for her ID. Without speaking or expression she took her license out. She wondered if liquor store clerks consider what is hidden behind the masks their customers wear when they come in at one o'clock in the afternoon to buy a fifth? She drove back to the hospital and parked in the back parking lot. She didn't even bother to open the soda. Still in its sack, she drank from the bottle: the Original American Medication. Liquid fire and acid burned her lips and tongue and throat. Bile threatened to come up as she choked on tears. "Oh fuck. I hate this world. I hate this life, this system. My gender, my history, my future - all fucking wrong." And so her head said, over and over, like a scrolling marquee.

She didn't know how long she sat there, but after awhile her head became quiet. The bottle was half-empty and she was warm. Chewing a piece of gum, she got out of the station wagon and walked toward the hospital. "No one needs to know," she thought. "It isn't like it is a big deal. People drink all the time; it's a socially acceptable practice. It's not like I am at work. It's not like I am breaking a commitment to anyone. Just for today, I will take a respite from the cold gray series of events life has become. Just for today, I can shut the fucking noise up in my head."

Not all events are life changing. But some are. Having an organ transplant is life changing. Getting sober for any period of time, after being in the grips of addiction, is life changing. Your mind and heart and soul are changed; and will never be what they were before sobriety, no matter what you tell yourself to the contrary. Recovery is a journey, not a destination. Sometimes relapse is part of the process. But Lena was confused. She thought it was the end of her recovery, and in a way, was a bit relieved.

Michael, himself sober for 18 years, had seen the path of destruction that addiction plows through peoples lives. He wasn't about to enable Lena to sit and spin in her own justifications. "What do you want me to say? That you should go to treatment? That you should not be doing this alone? That I can say."

"I think you should tell me I can drink in moderation. I think you should tell me whatever I want to hear. I think you should tell me to follow my own heart and live today. I think you should tell me I am too smart to stay at the table too long. That I know when enough is enough because I have had enough," was Lena's reply.

"A person's gotta do what they gotta do," he said, and walked away.

Nineteen

Butterfly, butterfly, whence do you come?

Lena got in the shower with a beer. She set the bottle on the ledge where the soap goes, and began to shave her legs. It was finally spring. A beautiful Saturday afternoon. The tulips and daffodils were blooming in the garden box. In her home everything was just right. Jerry was working in the garage, the children watching TV. She had the idea she might go visit friends for a few hours. Just for fun. No bars or anything like that. This wasn't the old days when she slutted around. She had a good life now. No one knew the girl she had been. She rinsed her hair then took a long drink of beer. Henry's. "It will make you fat again," Ellen's voice inside her said. "Fuck it," she answered back.

The beer gone, her legs and private parts shaved baby smooth, she got out of the shower and towel dried. In her room, she put on a new sleeveless dress. Eddie Bauer, no less. Then she called Cheri.

"Hey Cheri, what's up?"

"Nothing. Just hangin', listenen' to music. Wanna come over?"

"I guess. I got nothing planned yet."

"Okay. See ya then."

Lena went into the kitchen. Everything was in its place. She took the scotch from the cabinet above the stove. She poured it over two ice cubes and returned to the bedroom. Slipping on her sandals, she glanced at herself in the mirror. She paused. Her eyes were a bit glassy, and her hair hung in her face. Could that really be her? She looked so small, and worn. Even mean. "Best not look too hard girl," Ellen's voice came through. She went back to the bathroom and finished her face and hair. She swallowed two Darvocet's with the last of the scotch and closed the door behind her.

Down in the garage, Jerry saw her leaving. "Where are you going?"

"Over to Cheri's."

"Why?"

"Just to visit."

"Well, what about the kids?"

"You're here. Can't you watch them?"

"Yeah, but, you look so good, maybe I should come with you...you know, keep the guys away." He smiled slyly and reached to put his arm around her waist.

She got in the station wagon. "Well, if you want to see if Monica can baby sit, then maybe you can come over. I won't be long though, and we won't be going out or anything." Ellen said, "Shut the door!" So she shut the door.

Lena smiled at Jerry. "Okay, then. See ya later, maybe." He just stood there in the driveway, watching her back out.

At Cheri's they sat on the sofa passing the bong. First Troy, Cheri's boyfriend and dope dealer, then Cheri, and then Lena. Then they listened to music. Cheri was having trouble with the washing machine, and Troy got up to try and fix it. Lena wanted another scotch.

"Hey Cheri, you got any scotch?"

"Uh, no, I don't think so."

They had put the bong down. The phone rang. It was Jerry. He was on his way. Had it been that long? Lena wondered. That feeling of wanting to do or be anywhere other than with him came, and Lena stood up.

Troy yelled, "You want something, why don't you go out and get it, 'stead of coming over here and smoking all our pot. That's all you do."

Cheri was quick: "Don't be an asshole Troy. I invited her. Besides she bought it last week."

"Fuck you bitch."

Lena got up. "Yeah, okay. You want anything?"

"Some chips and beer would be nice," Troy said, walking up close to where she was standing.

"Hey, be nice, Troy. And can you get some bean dip?" Cheri asked. "I love bean dip."

"Wanna come with me Cheri?" Lena asked.

"No way!" Troy yelled. "Last time you guys went out to-gether you didn't come back till the bars closed. No way. Cheri stays here until you get back, then if we go out, we can all go. Jerry will be here too, so get him something he likes."

She got in the station wagon to leave. Jerry was pulling in. She smiled and waved. "Hey!" he yelled out the window. She just kept driving. She checked in the mirror to see if he followed her. Nope.

Driving high wasn't a lot of fun. She tried what she thought was normal, concentrating so intently, that she had driven all the way through town without realizing it. She was supposed to stop at the ATM and get money, and then go to the liquor store. She had passed all the banks and stores, and was in the east part of town when the cell phone rang.

"Hello?" Lena said.

"Hi, girl. It's Michael. Hey, I thought we were having cof-fee? Where are you?"

"Uhhh, hold on, uhh, okay. I am driving. I am sorry, I forgot about meeting with you."

"You forgot?" He paused, but when she didn't respond, he said, "Well, how about now?"

"Oh, well, you see, I've been given the job of finding an ATM and getting beer and chips for a party. Everyone is waiting for me. The thing is, I am having a problem getting to the ATM. I keep passing them instead of turning."

Pause. He let out a sigh. "Where are you? Pull over right now and tell me where you are."

"Okay. Okay. God, just give me a minute. I can't stop, there are people everywhere."

"What are you near?"

"I am going around the hill. There is no place to stop. Just stop yelling at me."

"I am not yelling. Listen; can you get to the bookstore? I'll meet you there if you will give me a few minutes."

"I really shouldn't. Everyone is counting on me, I can't just ditch them."

"Okay. No problem. I just want to see you for a minute. Pleeeeeaaase?"

"All right. I'll stop for a minute." She put the phone down. "What are you doing?" Ellen asked. "Fuck this, you don't need him." But Lena ignored Ellen, and carefully parked.

Michael pulled up next to her. He came over to her door, and she rolled down the window.

"I thought you were done with this? It's been five days girl. When is it going to be enough?"

"Did we really have an appointment? I don't remember an appointment."

"Yes. What happened?" He looked in her glassy eyes. She was not all there. He decided to just let it go.

"Let's go in for coffee."

"No. No, I don't think so. There are people in there."

"Yeah, well, it's a store. Come on." He opened her door and she got out.

They walked around inside for a while, then sat down at the Starbuck's counter and ordered coffee. The conversation was superficial and Lena kept looking around at all the people.

"Can we go now? It's just so bright in here. I can't stand the light. All these people are watching us."

"Okay, we can sit in the car and talk."

They went out to his van and talked for another hour. When Lena began to yawn, Michael asked if she was ready to go home.

"Never," said Ellen. "I despise that house, that home, that life, that game. Never."

"Yeah. I am getting tired," Lena said.

"How about going to the meeting tomorrow?" We can talk about this again then. You know, you don't have to do this to yourself. You have better ways of dealing with whatever it is that's eating at you."

She looked at him, and then stroked the side of his face. He was so beautiful, she thought.

She sighed, and got out and got into her station wagon. "I'll follow you through town," she said. And she did. It was a dark night, and very cold. Winter still had her breath in the air. Lena drove slowly, following his taillights. When he turned down his street, she kept driving. Then she stopped and turned around.

He opened his front door. "Hello. Did you lose your way?"

"No. Uh, I need to use the restroom. You know, the coffee and all. Do you mind?"

He hesitated, and then said, "Of course not." But he wasn't sure if he should be amused or concerned.

The house was dimly lit and a bit cold. She went in and used the bathroom. When she came out, she went over to the music rack and picked out *Super Tramp, Breakfast in America*. Placing it in the CD changer, she turned it on. Michael watched her from the sofa. Without a word, she walked back to where he was sitting. She looked at him through sleepy eyes, and then slowly straddled his lap. Her knit dress rose up to her waist. All the moments before this moment, every minute of every year before this moment disappeared. She paused and looked into his eyes. Michael slowly pulled her dress over her head, and then stood up, her legs still wrapped around him. He walked to the bedroom and closed the door.

He stood her in front of the mirror, wearing her panties and bra and sandals. From behind her, he wrapped his arms around her and looked at their reflection. Into the mirror, he spoke. "You are the most remarkable woman I have ever met. I can't just fuck you and walk away. I can't." Then, with the ease of the soldier he used be, he picked her up and took her to bed. He covered her in kisses until her body was pink, and her forehead wet with sweat. When they finally lay quiet, three hours had passed.

Disorientated, Michael looked at the clock. "Lena," he whispered, "you have to go home now." Nudging her gently, "You have to go. You can't stay the night. It's four o'clock in the morning."

She burrowed closer into him, and thought of her girls. What was she going to do? But she knew. She was going to go home, and then she was going to do what she had needed to do for a very long time.

Twenty

Baa, baa, black sheep, have you any wool?

Lena went home. Like other moments in her life, the clarity for change was urgent and all-inclusive. On that day, she knew, without a doubt, she was done with being a housewife. She was done with getting along with her in-laws, decorating and neurotically painting every room, every season. She was done with living the life she had created. She was done in the most insane sense, as if it were one of her paintings, or perhaps a long novel. Just done. For some people it may be hard to imagine this because in all cultures, all places and spaces in time, it is wrong to be finished with being a family, as if it were a meal, or a walk in the park. It is just not right to be done with your family, for no reason, other than it is complete, like finishing a puzzle.

Being done emotionally with your subscribed role in life, and the deconstruction of a life, are two different processes. Deconstruction generates the kind of disorder that people fear most in our culture. How can a person deconstruct their life without remorse, without apology?

That morning, back home in her own room, she cowered from the ideas that had come to mind a few hours previously. But there was no turning back. Once again, she had bought the ticket, and she was going to take the ride.

Lena climbed out of bed and put on her robe. Her body felt like cement.

She went onto the front porch where Jerry was sitting alone, drinking coffee.

"I'm leaving you. As soon as I graduate. I will get a job and find my own place."

"Again?" He smirked sarcastically. He had learned to predict Lena, and amused himself with being correct.

Lena didn't respond. They sat quietly on the porch until Jerry thought of something more to say.

"I know this is a tough time for you. I don't care what happened last night. I'm not even going to ask. To go back to drinking after 2 years must seem like a failure, but it's not." He paused.

There was compassion and hope in his voice. "The sober time has done you good. You lost all that weight, you're finishing college. It's what you think it is, not what those programmed alcoholics tell you. Change isn't failure. How long did you think you would go without drinking? It's a part of our lives, and that's okay, as long as you don't get carried away again."

Lena looked at him, wanting to laugh at the absurdity of his statement.

"You know, moderation," he continued.

Then she did laugh. But it was hollow. She had fourteen consecutive jobs her last year drinking. She fell down the stairs almost nightly. She had reached an unstable, 200 pounds of walking paranoia. Now, she was drinking again. This didn't bother him, but the thought of her leaving did.

"I finally have a bit of the old Lena back. You have been so demanding during your sobriety. You know what it's like for me, drinking alone? Wanting you to share life with me, but you are too busy cleaning or taking a class. All of your free time is given to the girls. If going back to drinking allows us to be together more, what's wrong with that?"

"Wow, what a ridiculous reality we have together," Lena thought. "I may not trust what I am doing or thinking, but I can't trust Jerry either. He has too much invested to see the situation for what it is."

"Okay, Jer, I know I am not making sense right now. I am really confused. I don't want to hurt you..." she paused, "but I have to leave." Her voice was confident. "I don't think I love you.

"You are a nice guy who deserves someone who loves you for who you are. That person is not me. I don't like who I am as your wife. There are women who would love the kind of husband and provider you are. I don't. I have tried to manipulate you; to change you into the partner I want. I am not willing to continue to behave this way toward you, and I am not willing to settle for anything less. I would rather have an empty space than be in a marriage with a person I am not passionate about. And you, why should you settle for a crazy alcoholic for a wife?"

Jerry glared at her. He had become accustomed to the mean bitch that followed an all-nighter. He knew if he humored her just a little, she would let out all the anxiety and come around to reality. She would cry and say she was sorry for saying those things, and promise to never leave. She always did.

"What do you have planned?" he asked.

"I know its sounds crazy, but I don't know. I just know that I need to do something completely different. Like… become a lesbian, and hike the Himalayas."

"Really? Okay," he chuckled, and then sighed. It was so far out of reality, he knew he was safe from it.

Jerry never got it; what it meant to live with a person in the fringe. It never occurred to him that Lena couldn't see her reality as livable. It never really dawned on him that the life they had created together was just not right, and never would be. He had accepted that she would always be out of step with the rest of society, but it was okay, because the American dream was always the best dream and she knew that.

"Is this so bad? Is our life so bad?"

"NO! No it's not. It's a great life. It's the life everyone wants. We have a beautiful home, two darling girls. You are a successful, dependable person. I just don't understand what's wrong with me. After two years in the AA program, I still cannot find any joy, any reason, for this life…I…I want to move on with my life… but I don't know why." She paused. She didn't know how, was closer to the truth.

It was clear to Jerry she was very confused.

"You're confused," he said softly. "Like I said, I don't care that you started drinking again. It's just not that important to me. I would rather have you here with me, drinking, than out their somewhere doing God knows what. Hey, you are okay. Everything is going to be all right."

Lena was quiet for a moment, and then she stood up. "There comes a point when I have to make a choice. I choose recovery. Not the sobriety that the last two years has been, but real recovery. I don't know what that means. I am telling you this because I don't want you to think that everything is just going to go on like it always has. I want recovery. I am willing to do whatever it takes."

She went back in the house, shaking. She got dressed to go to the meeting at the hospital. In her mind, it was her only hope, like the single thread you rely on to keep your button attached.

That evening Jerry came into the bedroom to get ready for bed. The stress of the day was thick in the room. Lena, in her completely self-absorbed way, asked if he would listen to her.

"About what Lena? I am tired."

"About us. About recovery. About me."

"It's always about you, isn't it?"

"Yes, it is. But I am beginning to understand that there is a way for me to grow beyond that. Please."

"Okay." He sat down on the bed.

Lena looked Jerry in the eyes and said, "I am not in control of my drinking. I have been drinking to avoid reality. I use alcohol as an emotional pain reliever. Addiction controls me."

"Wait, can I say something? Not everyone believes that crap. If you think that alcohol is the scapegoat for all your problems, that it magically is in charge of everything, you are nuts."

"I believe I have moved from coping the best I can with my obsessive-compulsive behavior to actively running from life."

"Running from what? You have no problems. You are a housewife. What is it that you could possibly be running from?" He paused. "This is what I see: going to meetings where drug addicts and alcoholics and criminals belong is fucking you up!"

"Sharing the struggles with others in the program brings me out of my head and opens my mind up for new ideas to come in. The walls I have built to hide my shame and denial do more than keep others out. They keep me locked inside."

"What battles are you talking about? It's all drama. Drama you need to keep going to make your life more interesting. It's always about you."

"I know you are frustrated with this. I've been living a child-hood battle, which is still alive, when it shouldn't be. I have issues I don't want to deal with, so I cover up my emotional pain and insecurities with drinking. I want to surrender to this fight and learn to live one day at a time, in reality."

"How do you know that these people are not some cult, huh?"

"It's just that I have struggled so hard for two years, and nothing in my life has changed, except I wasn't drinking. I feel like I have no soul."

"I know how you have struggled. It's just that you really don't have to any more. You are almost finished with college. With the kids in school, you can do anything you want with your career. I am so proud of you. You look great... you are smart. It's sad that you can't see past your bazaar childhood in order to have a good life. That's always been your problem. Not drinking isn't going to change that."

"Yes, that's true. But the daily compulsion sucks right now. If I give into it, I will just stay in that shit. It's that cycle of starting and stopping that I want to get free from. I hate the thought of living another day in that trap. This decision is what the program calls the first step."

"Oh, okay. It's back to the program again. Listen, you've spent over two years in the program and never came to any of this. Why now?"

Lena opened her mouth to speak, and then closed it without saying anything. She couldn't yet face the honest answer.

He went on without an answer from her. "I don't want any more of this. Either drink or don't drink. I don't care. What I don't want is some new doctrine telling you who you are. You are okay just as you are. Can't you be happy?"

"Didn't you hear me? I don't want to drink, but I am not happy unless I do."

"Okay don't then. Just...just leave me out of this! I feel like I finally got back a bit of the girl you used to be, and now you want to change. Haven't you noticed you are never happy, and you live to make everyone else get caught up in your unhappiness?"

"Yeah." Lena hung her head. "I know. But I want that to change. Please try and understand. This is confusing to me too."

Jerry began to get into the bed.

"Jer, I really think I want to sleep alone for now. I think it would be best if I moved my stuff downstairs. Please understand."

"No," he said. "I'll go." Jerry took his pillow, unplugged his clock. At the door he said, "Just don't think that not drinking is going to fix you. You have a lot more problems now than when you drank everyday. Don't think I am going to wait for you to figure them all out either." He left the room and shut the door. They never slept together again.

Two days later at a meeting she didn't just listen. For the first time Lena shares out loud to a room of strangers, her reservations about committing to a sobriety program.

"I am worried that I do not have the ability to be honest. I might think I am being honest, but I am just pulling the cover over my own eyes. I am afraid that I cannot ever know honesty, and therefore will never be free from addiction.

"I have used the program as a distraction to my addiction in the past, and I am worried that is all it might ever be. I can say that I see the need for my will to be replaced by the will of a power greater than my own. I know that in my heart and in my head, but I am afraid that I will not be able to take that leap of faith and trust.

"I think I am waiting for a lightening bolt; but in reality, I know I must just be patient. I hope that is the case. I am also worried that I will find recovery in the fellowship, but never learn to manage in the real world. I have seen and heard others who are in that position and I do not want that for myself. I do not know what to do with my reservations except take them to someone who has time in the program.

"I can ask for help and insight. I can allow other thoughts to work in my head, but this requires a trust I have never had, and I am worried that I will get hurt. I am not angry, like I have been all this time, I am filled with shame. It is one of my most painful places. Drinking has been my cure. I can smell and taste a drink, and it has been two days.

"This affects all areas of my life. My husband doesn't trust me- for good reason. I can't think correctly and I can't sleep through the night. I don't want to face who I am, my spirit, my desire to separate. I have failed myself.

"When I drink I am very happy and giving. When I don't drink, I am angry and abusive. I justify and rationalize my behaviors by saying that it is the only way I can cope with stress, with people and with my head. Today my life is reduced to compulsion, and knowing this simply brings more shame. "

It had taken 12 years for the illusion she believed would fix her, to run its course. It took twelve years for her to come to terms with the fact that having and loving children does not somehow make living acceptable. It took twelve years for Lena to give up on creating her own version of love. She just didn't know what she was supposed to do next. This- not knowing what to do- turned out to be a good place to start.

Twenty one

Hey diddle, diddle, the cat and the fiddle, the cow jumped over the moon

It took 43 days, but Lena made a decision and moved forward with it. Like her great grandmother who moved from Ireland to become an American, Lena moved from being a housewife to being a single mom. It was as if she hadn't just moved into a new apartment, but moved into a new person. July 3rd she was the crazy bitch who is leaving that poor man; and July 4th she was a new tenant on the west side, trying to raise two young ladies on her own.

When you choose to recreate a life, some things must go. There are those items that you can guess will no longer be needed. There are those places that you no longer frequent in the course of a day, week, and month. And there are faces you do not wish to see. The reasons vary. Maybe they are a reminder of who you do not want to be, or a certain place may conjure up memories of mistaken paths.

This process of elimination is not always simple. In the course of remaking a life, there are some items, places and faces that are not easily cast off, no matter how badly you may wish to rid yourself of them. At first they can simply be ignored. However, at some point the tremendous changes that take place in remaking a life create such contrast between the old and new, ignoring that which will not leave becomes impossible. This is Ellen.

It was Lena's inability to come to terms with her particular form of neurosis that created problems. On one day, Ellen was that confident voice that appeared unaffected by the catastrophe of her life. Ellen would be the guardian from her childhood and the voice of her mind. The next day, Lena believed Ellen wasn't real, telling herself that she was imagining things, making Ellen's words insufferable.

Real or not, Lena intellectually understood Ellen. She understood where Ellen came from. She understood that the purpose of the guardian has long been over, but that the voice still echoes fears from two decades earlier.

She confided in Michael one afternoon during lunch break, not sure how he would take the disclosure of such an insanity. He said nothing in reply. Embarrassed, she went back to work. That evening after her girls were asleep in their beds, Lena reads the following e-mail from Michael:

Dear Lena

There is a very fine line between brilliance and madness. The closer we come to fully realizing our potential, the louder the fear noise comes up to tell us we are going crazy. Visualize a clock face with madness at 11:59 and ultimate clarity at 12:01. Is it any wonder that our addict is happiest at 6:00; sedated and relieved of all stress and responsibility? So what is at 12:00? Perhaps the very fabric of the universe, passage to the next dimension, our fear, maybe love, maybe nothing. It is just my theory, but most of the really intelligent and insightful people I have known over the years have suffered with it. Many become violent; some commit suicide; some write about throwing it off the edge of a cliff to be rid of the conflict. Perhaps we look at the core of our spirituality, and are so unable to understand and control it that it freaks us out. I can only call it 'IT' because I have no label. But twice in my recovery I have climbed the mountain and have touched the sky. Whatever you call it, *IT* is very real, and the peace that flowed through me at those moments was more intense than any high, any orgasm, and any *thing*.

You are not crazy!
Your are not alone!
You cannot force this process, and you are too far along to quit.
You are not in charge.
You cannot control the outcome.

You will learn to LOVE,
And to forgive,
Starting with yourself.

Or as my sponsor, the reverend Motorcycle Ed said to me:
"Work the steps, or die, mother-fucker."
Choose life, your family, and love.
It is only the fear that is stopping you,
Or as Greg said: "lack of recovery"

Who was the sage who was asked to tell all the secrets of the universe, while standing on one foot?

Trust the process!!
And be gentle with yourself.

Love, Michael.

When you are innocent, you don't realize when you're being used. When innocence fades and awareness begins to seep into the consciousness, that knowledge can create an ugly wound. Ellen was that wound. A walking, talking, ball of rage. Her pure unpredictability made her difficult to have around. And dangerous. This was a bad time for Lena to have Ellen in her life.

In recovery, everything must change in order to live without the use of drugs and alcohol. In Lena's life, that meant Ellen must change also. As her internal guardian, and ultimate protector Ellen held much of the control over Lena's interpretation of the circumstances in her life. So when Lena saw Ellen on the bridge that hot July day, she had hoped for an outcome they could both live with.

How do you lose a person who won't get lost, and lives to torment you? There was no question in Lena's mind that Ellen had become a serious problem in her new life. There was no question that the girl had to go. The how of the matter, was the answer she searched for.

Michael gave his advice. "She is your friend," he said. "Your confidant, your sister. Meet her again, embrace her, and love her. You need her to be whole."

That hope disappeared on the Crooked River Bridge, as Lena watched Ellen fall silently through the air. Time seemed to go very slowly. The body was as small as a pebble when it hit the water. Gone.

Standing there she was not sure exactly what to do or feel. How does one feel at such a point? She sighed and turned around to walk back to the car. She wasn't sorry. Lena knew the iniquitous truth. Her internal guardian, with all her powers of disillusionment and control, may be gone, but Ellen was not.

It was time for her to go. It was time to get on with getting on. Back at the parking lot sight- seers were staring at her. She gets in the station wagon and took the keys and glasses out of her purse. Putting the glasses on and starting the car seemed oddly new. Lena pulled out of the park and onto the highway. She had some business to take care of.

Fear is the extreme motivator. It made Galileo recant, it secured Judas a place in history, and it drove Lena to remove herself from herself. With the internal guardian quiet, Lena was convinced that the young foolish girl who leapt to her death will never return, freeing her from the insanity of her past, and the fear of the future. With a new kind of abandonment, Lena set out to change her life, piece by piece. Unfortunately, not everything that troubled Lena can be removed, left behind, purchased anew, or sacrificed over a bridge. The real changes that come with recovery are gifts of a spiritual nature. Lena had issues with that.

Twenty two

In marble walls as white as milk,
lined with skin as soft as silk;

NOW is the space where the actors on the stage linger over the lines. They consult for direction, distraction is high, and the scene stumbles forward. Now is where Lena was. She was not happy with now. She sensored it, looking for unacceptable content. Trapped by previous scenes, she analyzed it and criticized it and believed somehow, if she were the director, a magnificent production would materialize in front of an astounded audience. Dramatic in her absurdity, she continued. Liberated from one theater, she rehearsed her lines in another.

Life on life's terms is often difficult to recognize for people in the fringe. Differentiating between the real and normal and the fantasies of the mind are difficult. Fringe people often struggle with choices they will never face in reality, and refuse to look at consequences of the choices they make every day. It is this difficulty that Lena struggled with, to mentally and emotionally stay on task with reality. But the reward for her effort paid off. She graduated from college, showed up for her single parenting responsibilities, held the same job for an entire year, and hadn't touched a drink in 13 months. All the while, Michael was still there, pushing her to grow spiritually.

"I heard this guy say in a meeting, that he never prays because he doesn't want God to know where he is and come after him to collect," Lena said one summer day, smoking and drinking coffee at their favored spot.

Michael looked at her with those gray eyes that never betrayed him.

"What is a power greater then yourself, Lena?" Michael asked.

"I know I am suppose to know this, that sobriety depends on this, but it alludes me."

"Start with the basic concept. You're getting ahead of yourself by trying to figure it out. Just answer the question: Is there such a thing as a power greater than yourself?"

"Yes. But in terms of how that power will impact my life, I don't know. I am not really sure. Light can illuminate a room, but you're suggesting a light that can illuminate a life."

"Could there be such a power?"

"Maybe. Yes, I suspect there is a spiritual power in the universe, but I do not know how to connect with it. I have experience with religious teachers, and the Jesus thing isn't for me."

"What would your higher power be, if it could be anything?"

"Anything?"

"Anything. What can you relate to?"

"Well, I guess if I were to envision a higher power, it would be a master gardener, and she would have all the knowledge of how everything works. She would speak to me in a way I can understand, and help me to understand those things in life that don't make sense right now."

"Like what?"

"Like how can I feel comfortable with being sober.? What is the right thing to do in wrong situations? When is it okay to speak up; and when should I just keep my mouth shut? Why do I feel separate from everyone? Why do I obsess over things I cannot change? How is my life going to work out, when it is such a mess? How can I see life clearly so I don't have to fall apart when something unexpected happens?"

Michael smiled at her. He didn't speak again until it was time for her to go back to work. "How would your life be different if you behaved as if there was a God working in your life, instead of wondering if there is?"

Lena looked at him. He was beautiful and ancient. Her lunch break from the bank was over; and she was gratefully free to leave the difficult conversation. They embraced and then departed for their separate destinations.

In recovery, a concept of a God will not keep you sober. Alcoholics must have a personal connection with a higher power to lean on in times of turmoil and disillusionment, or else they will return to the bottle for comfort. It was this knowledge that drove Lena to her knees to wait for God to show up.

In her small apartment Lena got on her knees. She leaned forward and cradled her forehead in the palms of her hands to keep her face from touching the carpet. With her eyes closed, curled up like a ball, she tried to think of nothing. Except nothing is something, so she decided to say the serenity prayer: "God, grant me the serenity to accept the things I cannot change, the courage to change the things I can, and the wisdom to know the difference."

Night after night she did this, with no enlightenment. Then one night, she was so tired, she began to fall asleep in this position. As she began to drift, she heard a soft female voice say, "Open your eyes." She sat up and opened her eyes. She was in her darkened room, the red numbers on the clock by her bed read 10:32. She got into bed. "Okay," she thought, "I am talking to myself. This is hopeless."

The next night, after saying the serenity prayer, she heard the voice again, "Open your eyes." So she did. This time though, she didn't sit up. With her eyes open she could see her forearms and the carpet. Maybe, she thought, I am supposed to pray with my eyes open. This didn't seem right though, because she became distracted by the slit of light coming through the bottom of the bedroom door, and got up and went to bed.

The following night Lena went to the closet to pray. She wanted to either know there was a spiritual power that she could connect with, or know that she was on her own. One way or another. In the closet, with the door shut, bent over with her head in her hands, Lena prayed.

"God, Highest Power of this universe, please talk to me. Please come to me. Am I a fool to keep calling for you? I don't want to be a fool, but I don't want to be alone. Where are you?"

Again, a quiet voice said, "Open your eyes." In the dark closet, Lena opened her eyes. At first all she could see was black. Then, a small dot of green light. The dot was slowly growing larger, until she could make out a patch of grass, some dirt. The circle continued to grow big enough for her to peer into, like looking into water. There was grass and dirt, and something.... Lena sat up quickly. The illusion disappeared, and she was in the dark closet again. Her legs had gone numb, but she was not ready to leave. She bent back over, put her head in the palms of her hands, and prayed. 'God, Greatest Power of this crazy planet, please bring me closer to you.'

"Open your eyes." Lena did not open her eyes, she opened her minds eye. There, as quick and easy as flicking a light switch, she was sitting in a garden.

Lena looked around. The circle of grass she was sitting in ended a few feet away, surrounded by tall delicate flowers. Further away she could see lilac bushes, trees of various sizes, and a wooden bench. Lena turned and looked over her shoulder to the right. The sight was not so pretty behind her. A mangled vehicle of unknown origin was only a few feet away. It was lying on its top, wheels in the air, windows broken out. It was consumed by rust. Lena turned back to the bench and the lilac bushes. Something had moved.

Lena squinted in the bright light. She thought she could make out the image of a woman sitting on the bench. She held still for a moment, wondering if she was intruding. Lena had forgotten she was in prayer.

Lena watched the woman for what seemed like hours. The woman was wearing a white gown that flowed around her. She had long light colored hair that moved gently around in the warm breeze. She would look down at something on the ground, then she would look over at Lena, then look back down at the ground. After what seemed like eternity, Lena decided to go over to her. Lena stood up.

The garden disappeared as quickly as it had arrived, and Lena was left standing in her closet, surrounded by her hanging dresses. Surprised, she just stood there. After a moment, logic and reasoning came back, and she realized she must have fallen asleep and dreamed the garden. She opened the closet door and got into bed.

The image of the garden sat in the back of her mind until the next evening before bed. She lingered over whether to go back to the closet to pray, caught between not wanting to believe but wanting go to the garden again.

Lena slid the closet door open and stepped into the small space. She nervously got down on her knees and slid the door closed. With her head in her hands she said the serenity prayer. Nothing happened. Then with all her heart, Lena prayed. "God of this universe, please bring me closer." Then she waited with an open mind.

Softly, but clearly, Lena heard, "Open your eyes." Without sitting up, without removing her hands from over her face, Lena opened her minds eye. She once again found herself in a patch of grass surrounded by tall flowers. Beyond her sat a woman on a wooden bench. The woman was looking at her.

Lena wanted to move but was afraid. Then she remembered how she opened her eyes, without physically opening her eyes. She thought she would try that. She would try to spiritually stand up. Nothing happened. She tried again. Thinking lucidly, "I am standing." She felt her body rise up. She thought, "I am walking," without moving her legs, she began moving closer to the woman on the bench.

Without taking a step, she made her way to the bench. A few feet from the woman Lena stopped. She looked at her. The woman was sitting politely, hands resting in her lap, bare feet on the ground. Her head was tilted slightly, and she was looking at Lena like she knew her, was expecting her.

"Hello" she said.

"Hi," Lena replied. There the conversation stopped. After a moment Lena asked, "Where am I? Who are you?"

"You are in your garden, Lena. I am… a spiritual sister. You invited me here."

"My garden?" Lena asked.

"Yes, this is your garden. Would you like to sit down with me?"

"Thank you," Lena said politely, a bit baffled. "You mean I made this all up in my head?" Without waiting for a reply, she continued. "Oh, I am really mental. I knew it."

"No, this is not a mental illusion. It is a real place out of the physical world. This is a place… between places. See, the spiritual world does not have the elements you needed in order to feel safe. So you have chosen to create this garden in order to meet me."

"Oh." Was all Lena could think to say.

They sat in silence. Lena looked around again. To her left the flowers stretched out to a hill, which rolled over the horizon. The sky was baby blue. To her right was the twisted metal vehicle lying on its hood. Surrounded by dirt and rocks, it looked out of place. In front of the vehicle was the patch of grass she had found herself on when she arrived.

"What is that?" Lena asked pointing to the wreck.

"You brought that with you." She said. "When you first began to pray, you were inside it, and couldn't get out." She looked at Lena and smiled. "I am glad you found your way."

Lena sat there thinking. "Can I come here whenever I want? All the time even? Could I just live here?"

The Sister looked at her sincerely. "Yes, but the garden would die," she said. "The garden is a spiritual reflection of your life. You and I have created it to give you a place to see what is happening in your life. You know how you have prayed for a guidance, for knowledge?" Lena nodded her head. "This is where you will find that reflection and knowledge. If you were to stay here, the garden would eventually die, because your life in the physical world… would die."

"But it's so beautiful…peaceful. Is the spiritual world like this in other places?"

"No, she said with a smile. "The spiritual world is much different. It is a place without time. It is everything good…. there is no passage to which a beautiful thing changes. There is no process of creation, as every thing that is good is finished."

"I don't understand that."

"That is why you are here. This is a gift from the universe to you. I will meet you here whenever you call. The health and beauty of this garden is a reflection of the health and beauty of your physical life. You can come here to find peace, to examine that which you are cultivating in the physical world, and to find comfort."

"Do you know everything about everything?" Lena wanted to find God.

"I know only what is true," she said.

"Can you tell me why I am unhappy so much of the time?"

"Because you were in that wreckage." She nodded toward the rusted metal heap.

"Am I going to be...okay?" Lena heard her voice quiver on the word okay.

"You are already okay, Lena."

Puzzled Lena asked, "Why do you say that?"

She looked into to her eyes. Lena could see a kaleidoscope of colors around the pupils. Her face had the soft lines around the eyes and mouth. Not old but not young.

The Sister took Lena's hands into her own. They were warm. She said to Lena, "You are okay because you made it here. You know, and you will *never not know*, that there is a blessed life for you."

Lena thought about this. "Thank you." She said. "I am..." she had wanted to say how grateful she was, but began to cry instead. She put her face in her hands and began to weep with gratitude. When she finished, she looked up, and found herself back in the closet.

Delusional as it may seem, Lena began a life long relationship with her spiritual guardian. Sometimes in desperation, sometimes for companionship, Lena went to her and the garden and always found comfort, and most importantly, reflection.

The garden gave form to all things that choked Lena in life. She examined every clump of grass, every hole, every rock, and every mound of dirt. Each item and its corresponding character defect in her real life were examined for its usefulness: fear, dishonesty, envy. She also found love, generosity, courage, perseverance. Those things that were complementary to sobriety, she thanked her Garden Sister for. Those things that made her want to get loaded, she asked to have removed from her life. Simple.

Not everything that is simple is easy.

Twenty three

Cut thistles in May, they'll grow in a day

For a period of several years, it was a seemingly uneventful life. Symbolic of the infectious nature of love, Lena grew a career and recovery as attentively as she nurtured her two children. As they grew, so did she. It wasn't in one day or one year, but over a string of years that Lena morphed from needy child to independent woman. It was through brutal honesty, and soft decisions made in faith, that those changes are realized. In the fringe the setting for this growth is called recovery. In God's world, the setting for this growth is called love.

With this love Michael writes:

To My Dearest, Dearest Lena:

You talk to me of fear:
I know the dark place very well
A lifetime in a box, safety by defense,
Keep them out, no one touches that place,
No one can come in.
Close, but not too close
Touch, but don't stroke.
Know the shell, not the inside
Fake it, Fake it, Fake it
Shut down, Shut out, Shut up.
Create situations to reinforce the beliefs,
Create beliefs to smother the situations.

You talk to me of trust:
Trust what?
Myself? Not a good track record.
Self-betrayal upon self-betrayal.
Others? Feet of clay,
Self serving interests,
Friends of convenience,
Lovers of lust,
Lovers of need,
Who only see fear.

Recovery:
A bright spot.
Train in a tunnel?
Hope to the hopeless?
Years of struggling against the flow,
Swimming against the current,
Refusal to accept the simple principles-
Damn-it, I want my way!
But the miracles keep happening, despite me.
Hard lessons, but they are remembered,
Sometimes even learned from.
And friends, who seem to want nothing from
me....but me???? Too strange.

So I stay, and learn not to listen to my head,
But to learn the definition of wisdom:
The gentle blending of the mind AND the heart.
Learn to listen for the quiet voice,
Not the screaming one.
And to believe in the divine design,
The path, the flow.
Trust that I am being guided,
That everything has a meaning
And to look for the messages.

And You:
My precious, precious beautiful Lena:
No need to explain the conflict, identical on our insides.
So powerful,
So frightening,
So intense,
So soft,
All encompassing,
Yet safe.
Connection, unlike any in past experience.
Inside each other's heads,
Inside each other's hearts.

Head screams "are you nuts?"
But I have learned not to listen to first words from my head.
Heart cries "you'll get hurt!"
But I have learned the heart can be governed by fear.

But the program has added another component to wisdom
Equation:
Soul.
A funny thing; soul.
Seems to temper the other two,
With a gentle hand.
Soul says, "this is different."
Door has opened, eyes of a child,
Wide with wonderment;
Amazing, just so amazing.
    Love, Michael

Even with his confession of love Lena had never felt so
alone; she had never felt so vulnerable. She was looking for recovery. She thought real recovery would be the cure that would
bring instantaneous satisfaction- like scotch. She still saw her
only freedom in that great state of Americana, was death. Poor

Lena. She had claimed her education, was gifted with employment, and struggled to show up for each new day, as time
advanced itself on her.

Pulling Lena closer to the center of reality, Michael knew
that truth was constant and unchanging; that it was the questions Lena sought. Michael reached Lena intellectually, with
love.

My Dear Intellectual Lover,

On disease concept:
The ultimate goal of the disease of addition is to self-de-
struct our lives. Many rationalizations, many excuses, many,
many poor me's. Watch a small child build a sand castle on the
beach. Hours digging, fussing, sculpting and detailing. Then
watch the smashing as the reality sets in of the impending loss
because of the trip back home. Or perhaps, just so no one else
can enjoy it.

This leads to the mental manifestation: the obsessive-compulsive nature of the addict. Anything that feels good must be
done to the point of extreme. Anything I don't have and want is
a maddening noise in my head. Life is made up of three reali-
ties: that which I must have, that which I cannot stand to lose,
and that which I must get rid of at any cost.

The physical is the symptoms: chemical dependency,
obesity and anorexia/bulimia, tree-hugging wacko's and right-
wing godlike assholes, spendaholic/miserholic, sexaholic and
hideaholic, control everything and be victimized by everything.
So many I can't count.

On Life and Death:
Do we pass through the medium that we have created in
this life? Do we live within our minds? Or am I a fingernail,

a limb, a heart, a gelled piece of meat called a brain? If I am inside a house, am I the house? If the house falls down and I leave, am I less without it? When I enter a car, the lifeless takes purpose, movement and direction. Does that make me a car? If the car can go nowhere without me, can I go nowhere without the car? Is the union of the two to find meaning and experience in the journey? Is thought real, and physical the illusion? What is true in our minds is true, regardless if we know it our not.

Love Michael.

Twenty four

Ladybug! Ladybug! Fly away home.

One day, not long after graduating from college, Lena realized that *it* had happened. A life. There it was. Lonely, oppressive in responsibilities, lovely in its difficult choices. Always a lesson for the learning. Autonomy. More of liberation. For the girl who wanted little, had found love in the corner of her life. She couldn't have imagined such a thing even if she had escaped to wild fantasies.

Fringe people who move into the fabric of society for employment find that the mundane, drone-like employer expectations are less then interesting. Maybe it is because of the constant crisis state of their previous lives that they find day-to-day activities trivial. Maybe it's because it is difficult to connect at a sales rally or staff meeting that spends an hour on the details of closing a sale on a $7 item. Maybe it's because fringe people haven't the same perception of what constitutes a priority. After all, a priority in the fringe is a crisis. Shelter, transportation. If you cannot get beyond meeting those needs, just about everything else takes a backseat.

Lena had an over developed sense of survival. In the past, it had served her well. But the point of Lena's recovery was to get beyond crisis management and the ridiculous desperation of clinging to her dreams, and recognize the journey of life could simply be a pleasant afternoon.

God herself issued Lena her first job in recovery. It was delivered in a perfect way at the perfect time.

Lena looked across the table at Michael. It had been a hard
day. Work as a teller is not anything like what she thought it
would be. She felt her failure was assured. Possibly because she
knew she needed it to survive, and so failure was instantly invited, and possibly because she was afraid of the main body of
society. You cannot get a much clearer picture of the social scene
then as a bank teller.

"It sucks to be poor," she said with a tired sigh over coffee.

"Hey, I gotta dollar. Wanna dollar?" He mocked her over-
dramatization of the situation. It was only coffee, after all.

The thought of a man contributing even a dollar to her life
brought up a collection of issues Lena was not prepared to face.
So, she got mad and left.

Still angry over Michael's perceived implication, Lena shared
in a meeting that evening. The topic was resentments, and Lena
vented twenty years of stuffed rage over her own behavior, to
a large group of individuals who listened without interruption,
without judgment.

"My name is Lena, and I am an addict and an alcoholic in
recovery."

"Hi Lena."

"I am ....I am mad at every fucking man who ever
gave a fucking dollar to any stupid fucking woman who doesn't
realize what she is selling, or doesn't care what she is giving
away. Mad that the culture is made up of fucking white male
pigs who dominate and stupid women who submit."

Lena took a breath and continued her explosion.

"Mad because social participation looks like the only sane, efficient option. Mad because social participation is fucking respectable for men, and so oppressive for women. Men do not have to choose between nurturing their children and nurturing their career.

"Mad because men expect women to nurture them. What do you think we are, endless suppliers of emotional support? Is the trade off - economic support? So it is some sick purchase thing that we call love?" Lena pauses, and looks around the room at the men.

"Men have all the power and then pretend that power is not the end game. That women should just accept powerlessness by default. I don't understand. Worse, I am not sure I want to.

"Resentments? Oh, I have resentments. I resent my parents for taking the easy way out of life by checking out emotionally. I resent my father for not providing basic life support for his children. I resent my mother for not protecting my sister and me.

"I resent society for treating me like a second class citizen because I was uneducated and poor. I resent trading twelve years of my life to a man I didn't love, for a home and a family, because I didn't know I didn't have to.

"I resent the American man for limiting God to Christianity.

"I resent my shortcomings, my lack of resources and my personal weaknesses. I resent alcohol for stealing time, money, love and honor from my children and family."

Then quietly, Lena said the most important thing: "I resent myself for falling short of who I want to be. Except I don't know who I want to be. I do know I don't want to belong to a man. That's all I got to say. Thanks."

"Thanks Lena." The group said in unison.

To this Michael writes:

My Dear Spiritual Girl:

I am just a man. I have done a lot of work on myself, but still suffer for all the defects that plague my own definition of 'Men are scum, women are bitches.' I ask you for your honesty, your guidance and your gentle nudges when I act or say stupid shit that devalues your whole person.

Mind reading is for normies. You tell me of the many things you find of value in me, but all relationships that progress beyond the honeymoon are based on honesty and mutual spiritual growth. I find you an incredible beauty, on all levels of this reality. Please, help me to polish these lingering traces of who I used to be. Know that I have as much to learn from you as you sometimes feel you want to learn from me. Unraveling can be painful, but breaking down the barriers is the whole purpose of this life.

I want to be the man you have waited for; the warrior that stands at your back; the soul you know sees all of you and is in awe of the power and beauty. I want a warrior too, not an object, not a 'thing' to bolster my ego, or to fill my needs. I want an equal, I want you, and I love you, all of you, as you are, were, and are rapidly becoming. Time is on our side, and slow but steady growth is a passport to what we have both waited for.

God is in charge; I'll just keep rowing and know that miracles happen around here all the time.

I just want you to know how proud I am of you. At two years the normal thing is that all of the props dissolve and many people decide that recovery is a lie, everyone just keeps saying the same old things, I should be able to handle social using, I'm bored with it all, etc. etc.

My two-year birthday followed my first spiritual awakening, as I faced financial ruin from retail therapy, and relationship hopping. I had done my damnedest to not feel, and to "get my life together" and of course it slipped through my fingers. For the first time I saw the difference from 'Just Not Using,' I had to let go of other people, look at my part only and trust something that I barely believed in would carry me through. The second step is called the leap of faith, and that is what it took for me to go forward.

Our journey can be a wonderful experience of joy and learning, or it can be a miserable clawing up the side of the mountain. We choose the labels and call the tune. Recovery is about how we live our lives, and how we interact with those around us, not about words we say.

Love, Michael

Twenty five

Lend me thy mare to ride a mile.
She is lamed, leaping over a stile.

Two years into her new life and the raw disfiguring process of recovery, the devil of Lena's childhood died. Web died of AIDS. It was, once again, a February day that brought change.

Lena and Jean had struggled to mend their broken relationship from the illness of Jeans son. Their conversations were painfully guarded. Lena felt shame from her behavior toward her only sister. Jean accepted her apologies, but was understandably cautious about what her sister was doing with her life. They saw and spoke to each other during holidays and birthdays. The biggest change was that they both respected each other for who they really were. Different, but equally valuable. They both struggled to do the best for their lives and their children's lives.

When Web died Lena and Jean decided to travel the three western states to attend his funeral together. They decided to enroll the assistance of Michael and his friend Steven to do the driving. It was a wise decision. It was a stressful time that didn't bring out the best in Lena. She was malicious and unstable. Jean was sullen and moody. For 20 hours they sat in the back seat of the car, talking about being sisters, about childhood neglect and abuse, and their rage and fears.

When they arrived at the cemetery, both women were no longer little girls. They were strong, vulnerable, courageous women. They did not speak to Elizabeth or Jimmy or any of the extended family. They simply laid to rest on his casket their rage and forgiveness, with their birth family and the universe watching.

On the way home, they slept. Exhausted, dazed, as February slowly rolled into March, and the new century saw its third summer.

Twenty six

Sing a song of six pense, a pocket full of rye

Recovery may be a spiritually based program, but it's nothing like American organized religion. Religious institutions are designed to provide a group of individuals with an experience that distinctly disconnects them from society, finding and replacing social values that are evil, with spiritual values that are righteous. Thus, the church member can be certain about the correctness of their life.

Recovery groups provide a member the opportunity to learn spiritual principles in order to relate *better* to society. Members in a recovery program examine not only substance abuse, but also the aspects of the addictive personality that keep a person from fully participating in society.

Lena had tried the religious experience, but it did not provide her with civic understanding in which to relate to family and community. While church leaders were quick to diagnose her self-centeredness, they treated her with guidance and direction that sustained her separation from the main fabric. The condemnation of society's evil ways only perpetuated Lena's separation from the main culture.

Finding recovery was like walking out of the dark. Growth through self-examination, fearless honesty, and a willingness to trust the process, was all that Lena needed. She need not subscribe to an ideology of sin. She need not be born again. She need not rely on the judgment of a moral organization to find answers to life's most pressing questions.

Women Soul is a recovery group Lena attended every week. There were other groups as well, but none as important as WS. Only woman attended, and they talked about, meditated on, and visualized, what it meant to be a woman. Each member established an area of her spiritual path she wished to focus on. For one year, she would keep that topic in front of her by sharing her experiences.

For Lena, the topic that year was obvious. She asked to have her authentic-self revealed through experience and meditation. Each week, members talked about the growth or lack of growth in that area, and received encouragement and strength from the other members.

The group met once a week at a community center building. It felt more like a lodge. Locked to the public during the weekend, it was private enough to feel safe. The large room held a kitchen, children's play area, and a fireplace. In front of the fire were sofas and recliners. The windows provided a view of a small playground and natural landscaping of Central Oregon. It was a comfortable place to speak your mind and heart.

The group of women were an ordinary slice of society. If you looked around the circle of women, you wouldn't find anything extraordinary. They looked like women you would find at the library, at the park with their children, or standing in line at the theater. Studious, quiet, absorbed in thought. What was special about them was that they all showed up to learn from each other. Previous experience of their own creation had left them disconnected and unhappy.

Recovery groups all have their own format. The WS group chose to read the 12 steps of recovery, the 'just for today message,' and then worked on individual topics. The guidelines were simple. Only one individual could speak at a time, they had to introduce themselves, speak honestly about themselves and their own recovery. To close they would embrace in a circle and say the serenity prayer. Simple.

"My name is Sharon, and I'm an addict."

"Hi Sharon."

"Well, I know what you're saying about wanting to take over and do things for my family. I've been free from my prescription narcotics for 93 days now." She paused while everyone applauded and congratulated her. Then she continued. "It really was by accident that I got hooked. I never set out to become dependant on painkillers. Now that I don't have the prescription to numb my feelings readily available, I get resentful of stuff that didn't bother me before." The group sat silent for moments, while she considered whether she wanted to continue.

"See, I am the house keeper, secretary, spiritual leader. I feel like I have to do all the planning, all the bills, all the shopping, all the cleaning, and all the relationship work. I write the letters, return the calls, and insist on church. If something is not my direct responsibility, I am right there reminding my husband what his responsibility is, because unless I do it myself, or nag him, it doesn't get done. Like you Lucinda, I have two grown children at home. They are strong Christian children; in fact, our home is a Christian home. I mean... I couldn't have it any other way. I love Christ, I think a Christ centered life is the most important thing a person should have while alive."

She paused. The group sat in silence.

"You know," she continued, "I am not sure where I am going with this. It's not like I'm unhappy. My problems are not bad at all compared to a lot of people. Sometimes though, I get so tired of being the strong one. When I got married, I thought I was getting a partner... or at least a companion..." Her voice trailed off. She didn't seem to want to continue with that thought.

"I had been divorced from my first husband for 14 years, when I got remarried. I had raised both my children on my own, had my own home. I had a full time career, a beautiful home, and a wonderful church family. Maybe I'm just getting old and tired, and want more help or less work. One or the other! I guess I need to just look on the bright side... what bothers me is that I don't remember feeling this way before I became addicted, and nothing in my life has really changed, so why am I feeling this way now?"

There, she said it. The words echoed in Lena's head, 'and nothing has really changed, so why am I feeling that way now?' There was something very important in that question.

It wasn't that Sharon didn't know her own heart or mind. It was that she did not want to face it. There was something, a sliver of something, creating inflammation, and she wasn't sure if she wanted to go through the pain to dig it out. So she didn't.

"Well, anyway, I am glad to be here, I am so glad to not be using meds. I felt so much guilt all the time. That's what I am free from. Guilt. Thanks for listening to me ramble."

"Thanks Sharon."

Lena didn't share, because Lena didn't know. But Sharon's words stayed with her until the next week.

"Hi, my name is Lena, and I'm an alcoholic."

"Hi Lena."

"I don't usually share," she said in a quiet voice. "I never know what to say, and I'm afraid I will reveal something I will regret later. I spend a lot of time thinking."

Lena let out a big sigh. "I'm not happy. I don't like my job, and I don't know why. I am very uncomfortable at work, and I don't know why. I work at a bank. It's a really nice bank. Everyone is very nice to me. And they are all women, and they are all beautiful and nice. I'm confused by my feelings... why am I so uncomfortable all the time?" She let out another sigh.

"I try really hard to fit in. I am nice to people, and I wear nice clothes. I don't swear. I don't complain. I always do what I'm supposed to do, without being asked. I feel proud of the work that I do." She paused.

"The thing is, I feel like I am made of plastic. Like Barbie's little cousin or something. Like nothing is *really* real. My sponsor said it's a normal feeling after drinking for fifteen years. She is probably right. I think that while I was drinking, I was hiding. Maybe it's like my eyes are adjusting to the light after being in the dark for a long time. Instead of it being my eyes, it's my feelings. Even at the grocery store, I get the freak-outs!"

A few women nodded their heads and laughed knowingly.

"I am impatient right now. I want to leave my job, this town, and the planet. I want to just get away. I don't want to deal with my issues. I have issues with my issues!

"I know moving will not change *me*. For me to find any kind of peace or joy, I know that I need to deal with the wreckage I have made in my life, and ask a higher power to change the way I interact with the new life I do have. My friend asked me what

I have to gain by believing that it is easy. I keep thinking about that. I always think everything is difficult. How can I think anything else? I can't just tell myself what to think. Can I?

"It helps to be around other women. To just get comfortable and let down my guard. Okay, maybe just get comfortable. Thanks."

"Thanks Lena."

It is easy to see the miracles that happen in recovery, because the members bring them to the meetings and share them without ego or arrogance. Being humble is a spiritual principle of the program. It is equally easy to see the ridiculous waste of energy members spend on absurd lives that deliver nothing but drama and pain. This is because members are honest and open minded, even with self-delusion. There is no better example of this then Sharon's story.

At meetings Sharon speaks about the circumstances in her life as if she had followed a recipe for chocolate cake and created glue. She was surprised and indignant that her efforts and resources were wasted on the situation, as if she had no responsibility or choice.

Her story began four years earlier when Sharon married a man who had been hurt badly by the woman of his dreams. Being the good person Sharon is, she knew she could restore his faith in women.

After the meeting, Lena asked Sharon if she wanted to talk some more about her crisis. It was unusual for Lena to have the kind of confidence it takes to listen and speak with someone on a personal level. But she had grown a bit, and she believed women need other women to ask them the hard questions and challenge the social programming that keeps them locked in unhappy, un-fulfilling roles.

They waited for the room to clear out so they could speak quietly and without distractions. Lena was nervous, because she knew in order to serve this woman she had to ask questions that would be difficult for Sharon to hear.

"I can only share my experience." Lena said and paused to think. "It has been my experience that victims, even victims of circumstances, are never out of material. What I mean by this is that I have in the past, and sometimes still, live in crisis from the acts of others. It is impossible for me to see that it is actually my inability to accept personal responsibility that I create my own problems."

Lena recalled the woman who had challenged her three days before her wedding, and drew on that example to press Sharon to think independently. "Ask yourself Sharon, what can you do today, to be true to yourself as a woman and a mother, and still respect your husband for his own... unique way of managing... or not managing, his life?"

"I don't know," she responded. "I don't see this about being a woman, or about victims. I know why my husband is not able to give as much as I need. He was unfairly wronged, and he is unfairly having to pay the price for his previous bad marriage."

"Then ask yourself Sharon, if your husband were to remain a victim of that circumstance, like so many people in this world, are you willing to spend your life trying to heal him?"

To this Sharon replied, "Do I have a choice? I married him."

Twenty seven

**Peter Piper picked a peck of pickled peppers.
A peck of pickled peppers Peter Piper picked.**

The day of her job interview she supposed she could pass
for a standard person. She got up early and straightened
her wide, frizzy hair. Then she removed the blue polish
from her short nails, and dressed in beige. Her Goodwill pantsuit
was tidy. It was the only suit she owned and was too large. It
swallowed her short frame, but made her feel proper. She drove
to the capital city early and waited in the hall of an undeclared
gray building. The secretary gave her the interview questions
and told Lena she would be called in ten minutes. Lena thanked
her and swallowed her panic.

This was just one of the many interviews that year. Lena had
been fired from her second banking job, ten months prior. After
a long period of self-pity, she began the process of applying and
being rejected, for numerous positions.

It was late fall and a window across the hall allowed the colored leaves on the trees to wave to her. Lena suspected the trees
outside knew why she was there, and they smiled in their beautiful dying way. I love the fall, she thought, and looked down at
her feet. Her shoes were a dirty brown. She tucked them under
the chair. She turned her attention to the sheet of questions. The
sound of blood pounding in her temples drowned out all thought.
It was hopeless. The questions didn't make sense.

A person came out of the room next to Lena. He was dressed in a gray suit. His shoes were a shiny black, and he looked like someone who might work for the IRS. But this isn't the IRS, Lena thought. The women who had handed her the questions reappeared.

"You can go in now Ms. Moran."

Lena rose stiffly, and walked mechanically into the room. As she entered she reminded herself, 'you are not twelve years old, and this is not the principles office.' "Thank you God," she mumbled as she closed the door behind her and took a seat in front of seven suits with people in them.

The row of seven people sat across the table from Lena. The woman in the middle introduced herself. She had an British accent. She explained the process of introductions, questions from the panel and then any questions Lena might have. Her blue eyes looked at Lena gently and her voice was warm. She paused for a moment. Her smile told Lena to relax and her blue eyes told her she would have the job if she could keep the remnants of the fringe from appearing in the conversation. At that moment, Lena relaxed. She knew it was okay. The leaves on the trees outside drifted gently to the ground, waiting for the street sweeper to suck them up.

After the interview Lena called Michael from the car and told him the good news. She had got the job.

"Just like that?" he asked.

"Well, no. But I know I got it."

"Oh. How?"

"There was this British woman who told me with her eyes not to worry, that I got the job."

"Oh, Lena. This is such a difficult process. Please don't..."

"You don't believe me?"

Michael took a moment to answer. Then he said, "Yes I believe you believe an British woman told you telepathically that you got the job. I guess I should just say Congratulations!"

"Thank you," Lena said triumphantly.

And so it was that Lena was offered a job in social services.

The women with the British accent at the interview turned out to be her boss. Her name was Laura, and she gave Lena the capital city tour, and introduced her to people she would never meet again.

At 5 p.m., Lena's feet were tired, and her hair had frizzed out so badly, she looked as if she were ready to appear on Saturday Night Live. But she didn't mind. Laura used the most entertaining British expressions. And the capital city was so beautiful. It seemed all the darkness of her life was no match for the city.

The agency loaded her down with portable data equipment. She drove away with an honorable assignment, and all the tools she needed to complete that assignment. It was up to her though, to make it happen. She drove from the state capital thinking she held one of the keys to rural services in the great state of Oregon.

On the drive home Lena imagined all the clients she was going to save from the streets. Those who are homeless, living with HIV and suffering under discrimination that Lena believed she understood. Her assignment was to locate social inequality, poverty and illness, and do something about it.

The fringe and the fabric of society react differently to mental and physical illnesses. If you live in the fringe and have HIV, you learn quickly that you must hide it. If exposed, you may loose housing, employment, healthcare, family, friends, even your life. In the fringe, ignorance is an ally of HIV.

Not true in the main fabric. The main fabric of society finds itself privileged to reach out and support, encourage and love the individual with HIV, as it is the kind of charity that may be used as a testament to social compassion. On the fringe, social compassion cannot compete with housing, food, and employment. The needs are too great to waste on such a frivolous use of energy.

The opposite is true for drug addiction, alcoholism, sexual deviance, and eating disorders. In the main fabric of culture, these issues find a most excellent place to hide. If you live and work in mainstream society, you must hide these problems, or risk losing your position. After all, even outside the church, society finds these issues a moral failing. What person would expose themselves to the ridicule and fear, by admitting to the moral corruption of these particulars? The opposite is true in the fringe.

In the fringe, addiction, alcoholism and compulsive/obsessive and destructive behaviors are courageously faced through admission, support and the willingness to not allow these diseases to live and destroy ones life. In the fringe when addiction is uncovered, it is a seed from which recovery can grow and change a person's life. Not just one person's life, but also all the lives that person has around them are changed for the better when an addict or alcoholic faces the disaster their life has become, and reaches out for support from a group. Self-help programs grow and thrive from the attendants who live on the fringe.

Where you are and what you are willing to do to maintain your position is what is important. Knowing the difference between unwritten social rules that govern deviance, and the main road of America, can save you from being a social outcast.

Lena's assignment was to become a part of an agency that resembled a department store, except it was a social service agency. She was to work in a government building with other agencies that serve the poor, unemployed, addicted, disabled, hungry and homeless populations of the great state of Oregon. It was called a one stop interagency connection. If you are hungry, you can meet with the food program representative. If you are looking for a job there are people from the employment department, job corps, area business council and temp agencies.

If you are in need of education, you will want to see Sandy. She can help you understand the community college and state college systems, what financial aide and scholarships are available for you, and of course, someone will help you fill the paperwork out. If you need housing, mental health, immunizations, English language classes, job application classes, personality profiles, senior services, disability services, unemployment compensation, public legal counsel, HIV information, fair housing info, and on and on. The list is endless, because the government was here to lend a hand with the problems that come from difficult situations in life.

The public who visits this building bring with them the specific identity that gets their needs met. The hungry bring their children, the disabled bring their cane, neck brace, and personal attendant- and they use the elevator. The non-English speaking bring their confusion, and the unemployed bring their resume. The poor wear sad eyes and grungy clothes and the veteran wears his honor and rage. The youth bring their naive sincerity. All go home with a little of what they sought, traded for bit of self worth and pride. That self worth and pride they leave behind now belong to the case manager who is then able to see herself as uniquely valuable to society.

Lena was the housing official for persons living with HIV. She liked her office. It validated her egocentric need to prove she could be successful even while playing host to her own personal demons. The office was anchored firmly in the fabric of society. Lena's clients never came to her office.

Lena's clients were the individuals who are discriminated against because they have HIV. These clients have nothing to trade of value. They live with a monster that is slowly devouring their lives. The people who surround them watch this process unfold and make their judgments, dishonor and betray them. In America, this invisible monster is like a scent that permeates throughout society. You get so use to being around it, you no longer smell it.

None of Lena's clients deserved the life they were living. No human being did. Yet her days were filled with their struggles.

A woman with two children working full time, had to choose between paying her health insurance and paying her rent.

A homeless man living in his car, too sick to make it to a bathroom. Health officials worry.........

Twenty-four hours before release, the penitentiary tests an inmate and declares him HIV positive. It isn't a coincidence, the facility cannot afford his medication, and so they turn him loose on the street.

Police demand an intravenous drug offender be housed so the facility won't be blamed if he becomes a public health risk. No public housing or low-income housing program will allow him to rent because he has felony drug conviction.

Mother of three, victim of domestic abuse, living in a motel is looking for suitable housing near a school. She has no income, and needs medication. Once tenancy is secured, her children are denied sport participation, the school is worried the uninfected children will pass the virus to others. The mother decides to home school.

Twenty eight

Little bunny Foo-Foo hopin' through the forest

When every issue during the work-day is a crisis, you learn to stop responding with alarm and start prioritizing 'situations.' Even the most extreme circumstances, such as a mentally ill guy wired on crank, threatening to kill her if she does not pay his rent, barely rates a nod. This was part of the learning curve Lena had to go through in order to keep her sanity and work with her clients.

Lena placed the individuals she worked with in three categories, not because they belonged in such an impersonal compartment, but because she could not make sense of their lives in any other way. In Lena's mind her clients were the socially neglected, the socially feared, or the socially criminal. Each client or family needing services fell into one of these categories, requiring a unique perspective and set of rules in order to assist them without wasting program money.

Of the 125 families Lena assistance, the socially neglected were the largest category. They encompassed a variety of individuals with barriers to living healthy lives. They included a culture of poverty where self-sufficiency was just beyond grasp, and rarely reached for. It included people who were so afraid of being stigmatized and shamed for having HIV that they delayed accessing medical care until they were acutely ill.

Then there were the socially feared individuals who could not access mainstream services because of the entrenched social bias toward the impoverished, single parent. Immigrants, refugees, ethnic groups, women, homosexuals, the poor, disabled and homeless.

Last, were the socially criminal who use meth labs, HIV medication, medical marijuana prescriptions, and the social programs, as there primary economic resource. When sustaining criminal activity is the only life you know, criminal thinking is instinctive. So is everything that comes with criminal thinking: isolation, fear and paranoia.

What she didn't know when she accepted the position in a housing program for homeless persons with HIV, was that the program was viewed as the bastard step child of a multi-million dollar state agency. They neither assisted with, nor cared to hear about, the challenges Lena or the other housing coordinators faced. By the second year of the grant, the program had burned through six employees, and was limping along with only two staff members. All Lena had wanted was to be a part of something good. In the end, she was the outcast representing the outcast. A mediator for the fringe.

The communities Lena worked in were the same rural setting she grew up in. Ranching or farming communities that had changed since the 1980's canceled the timber industry and made small business owners and gas station attendants out of loggers.

Lena tried not to internalize any of the crises her clients faced. She knew from experience that she must focus always on solutions to the problems. If she got caught up in the suffering, she would join them. But the stress begins to show in her dreams.

She woke up from a bizarre dream about pills. In it, she dreamed she was responsible for serving medication to people at a camp. The camp was in a thick woods and had a circle of small cabins, with a ring of rocks in the center, containing a small fire.

She set on a stump with her bag of prescription bottles. Lena took out a pill and sat it on a stump next to her, then smashed it with a rock. Then gently swept the pill dust into a medical cup and added a spoonful of applesauce. She then placed the cup on a tray near her feet. She continued to do this in the dim firelight.

Sometimes though, during the smashing process, she would drop a pill into the dirt. When that happened, she would pick it up and put it in her pocket. After awhile, a group of women began to form around the campfire. They looked familiar to her as they conversed between themselves.

Lena recognized many of the faces from her earlier years. Women who didn't like how she looked or acted, and told her so. Bold girls from the middle school and high school who talked in whispers, but never directly to her. The woman supervisor who tried to cry when she fired her from the bank, but just couldn't call up the emotion. Another was a customer from the bank who told Lena she smelled like cigarettes. Each one came to get their mashed pill and applesauce.

Now all the pills were gone and everyone had their medical cups.

It was then that Lena realized that she had someone's pills in her pocket. Who did they belong to? Would anyone notice they were missing? As she thought about this, a riot of yelling began as the women became her accusers. Someone in the group had died because Lena withheld their medication. Lena listened in horror and put her hand in her pocket. The pills were in there, and the group knew it. They continued to scream at her, accusing her of theft, addiction, and murder.

Lena woke up. She felt sweaty. She opened her eyes slowly and the dark room filled her view. The white net canopy and its rose trim could be seen in the blue night-light. At the foot of the bed, a white fluffy cat raised its head from the white bedspread. She looked at Lena, then got up slowly and came over to her. She lay at Lena's side and quietly purred. The dream was over, but its remnants of shame and confusion remained.

Twenty-nine

X, Y, and tumbledown Z,
the cat's in the cupboard

Rural Oregon was a vast place, and Lena traveled hundreds of miles to see clients. She was the only person in sixteen counties that helped homeless people with HIV find housing. She drove 40,000 miles her first year. With so much time behind the wheel, and nothing to do but think, Lena reflected on the nature of HIV, and its spiritual counterpart: Greed.

HIV is a brilliant disease. It infects, grows strong, immobilizes good cells, then sits back and lets a secondary infection destroy the body. People don't die of HIV. They die of illnesses their body cannot fight.

Like HIV, greed is a disease, a market disease. Capitalism has systems in place that keep the highly infectious gluttony of individuals from destroying a company from within. But sometimes, greed makes its way in through an unsecured window or door and paralyzes the safeguards that protect the private corporation. Once paralyzed, opportunistic fervor takes over: inflated profits, insider trading, labor exploitation, outsourcing.

Lena imagines HIV and greed are from the same batch of surplus waste rejected by the governing council of hell.

Lena is not alone in her work with homeless people living with HIV. She is part of a five-member group, each with a different region in the great state of Oregon.

Her team members are David, Angie, Jane and Laura, the manager of the program and Lena's boss. Every month they spend two days reviewing client issues and solutions. The issues revolve around the barriers clients face when trying to access mainstream social services. Most had been denied disability assistance, were unemployable, had criminal history and were too ill to advocate for themselves.

After Lena's program had been in place for a year, the Department of Corrections came up with a plan. Backed by public policies that encourage religious institutions to work in social services, the Oregon Department of Corrections decided to set up a program with churches to release inmates directly into the congregation in the community. Upon release, the ex-offender would live with a volunteer in the church community, who would watch him closely, and report back to the parole officer if there were any parole or probation violations.

In a meeting with the Department of Corrections, Lena expressed her concerns with the new program. As most of her clients were ex-offenders, she was concerned about the church knowing the status of HIV clients, and how that might compromise their right to privacy. To this matter, the clergyman from the Department of Corrections stated that all persons who wished to be assisted in finding housing through their program with the church, would have to sign a release of information that included everything about the convict, not just the persons HIV status, but also the information given during confession. This information would be transferred to the church member volunteer to use in assisting the homeless, ex-offender living with HIV to become a better member of society.

In response to this information, Lena pinched herself to make sure she wasn't in another bizarre dream. It just didn't seem right that citizens of a religious disposition should be asked to be quasi-probation officers in order to serve the homeless. It seemed to Lena that the Department of Corrections was in bed with the church and the religious community did not know it was being fucked.

This was not a popular metaphor to express, but Lena did anyway.

Thirty

There was an old woman tossed up in a blanket Seventeen times as high as the moon.

It had been four years, one month and eighteen days since Lena had a drink. It had been four years to the day since Lena moved into a new life of her own. Her two beautiful teenage daughters were now in middle and high school. She had seen professional success and failure. She had graduated college, bought her own small home, and most importantly, she had learned to listen for spiritual guidance. Now it was her turn to share this experience, strength and hope to an audience of recovering alcoholics and addicts. It was July 4th, 2003. It was the Friday night meeting.

The request had come two weeks earlier. She was sure it had been a set up by Michael. He had a connection with the secretary of the meeting, and fixed it somehow. In recovery though, when a request for service is made, you are required to give it full consideration, and Lena found no reason to say no other than she was terrified of speaking to an audience. Not because she was shy, but because she felt she hadn't the spiritual insight to deliver a message that would be of value to another in recovery. The only way to alleviate her fears was to pray and watch for signs as to what message was to be delivered.

First thing Lena did was try and write out her story. After eight pages of early childhood neglect, she gave up. Then she tried speaking into a tape recorder, but when she heard herself speaking it was such a boring, self-indulgent story that she stripped the tape out of the cassette. She then called her sponsor for advice, and talked about her fears at the woman's meeting. The answer was always the same, "God will do the work, you just show up. Watch for a message, and pray. God will let you know."

Faith and trust had always been Lena's biggest challenge.

In recovery, speaking about your experience, strength and hope is a process that delivers as much growth to the speaker as it delivers to the audience. It provides a necessary transition place of acknowledgement and release from the past, and offers opportunity to publicly solidify commitment to spiritual principles. Intellectually knowing this, Lena prayed for its delivery.

That Friday Lena knew the only thing she had control over in the event was what she was going to wear. With both daughter's at her side, they combed the aisles of the Goodwill superstore, to find just the right dress. They found a Tommy Hilfiger summer dress. It was white, with blue and red diagonal stripes and accents, that gave it a patriotic look. The princess cut fit well on her slim waist. The disco hem and clear shoulder straps gave it a perfect performance look. It was eight dollars. They paid at the counter and went back to the trailer park called home.

Michael and Lucinda were sitting in the carport, drinking Diet Coke and smoking cigarettes.

"Hey, what are you guys doing here?"

"I thought you might like some company," said Lucinda. "Besides, what else would I be doing on a Friday afternoon, but hanging with my favorite sponsee."

"And I came to see if you would like to ride to the meeting in my bus," Michael said and pointed to the motor home parked in the street in front of the house.

"Why'd you bring the motor home?"

"Well, I just thought it would be nice for you to have some privacy before the meeting, and then afterward we could stay for the fireworks. The girls could take blankets up on the roof of the bus to get a better view. I was also thinking… that the girls might want to watch a movie during the meeting…"

"Oh. Yea. I'm kind of nervous, it might help knowing the girls are not listening to me, you know, because I am momma when I am around them… and I censor what I say…" Lena said quietly.

"Of course you do. Do you know what you're going to share?" Lucinda asked.

"No. I tried, but nothing I've practiced seems right. I'm beginning to feel sick to my stomach."

"Well, that's not going to help. We have two hours for you to get ready and have something to eat."

"Well… I thought we could just eat there, at the BBQ."

"As long as you eat something." Lucinda was like that. Always thinking in practical terms. Her motto was 'do what you can, and leave the rest to God.'

So they packed the motor home with hot dogs and ice cream, and made their way through town to the meeting place. It was at Community Church activity hall that was rented out to various organizations during the week. It was a pretty spot. Built on a low hill, it overlooked the town. Best of all, it would have an amazing view of the city's fireworks show at 10 p.m.

The meeting began promptly at seven. The BBQ was not over, so people just brought their plates in from outside, and found seats at the tables. In the auditorium were 30 tables with six or so chairs around each one. Lena looked around. All the tables were full. Everyone was saying hi, and good luck, as they passed by her.

"My name is Lena, and I am an alcoholic and addict in recovery."

"Hi Lena."

A long pause followed this greeting. Lena was staring down at her shoes. She looked sincere and calm. Her hand holding the microphone was manicured. No ring was there. She was slim, with a full mouth and large brown eyes. Her hair was dark with long strands of clear white mixed in. It looked a bit like fishing line.

"Wow, there really is nothing to do up here but talk."

The audience laughs.

She joins them with small laugh. A secret smile. Where does a person get a smile like that?

Lena began, "It's kinda like praying. When you're down on your knees with your forehead on the floor. You know, with your hands in front of your nose and mouth so you can't smell the stinky carpet... and there's nothing to do but pray."

Laughter.

"So here I am." She looked up, and then quickly put her head back down.

"And there you are."

Laughter.

"I guess I should tell you that I haven't prepared anything, and that I haven't anything to deliver." She paused. The room was stone silent.

"I went through a process before coming here tonight. It was suggested that I write. In recovery, it's important to do what is suggested. So I wrote..... for several days. When I read what I wrote, I tore up the paper, and then put it through the shredder. I was not going to have those details ever be put on paper again."

She paused.

"I travel a lot for my job; so it was a natural suggestion that I speak into a tape recorder, you know, get comfortable with speaking. When I replayed my conversation, I realized I had spoken for three hours, and had not arrived at the first grade. The sound of my own voice, and the words I was listening to... well it was such a shock that I not only threw the tape away, but I pulled out all the ribbon first, just to make sure it was never to reach another ear."

She paused again. She was still looking at the floor, the microphone in hand, her mouth brushing the top of it when she spoke.

"I only saw two choices. Call and cancel this service commitment, or ask God for guidance. See, I wanted God to tell me what I should do, and how I should do it. I didn't get that. But

I was shown, very clearly, simply, what was the cause of my frustration."

"I was driving along the Oregon coast highway with my youngest daughter Faith. We were on our way to a path that runs along the cape. We were hot and thirsty, and we got out the soda we had with us. But it was warm, so I stopped at a roadside stand, and got a free cup of ice. I'm cheap like that."

Laugher.

"Back in the car, we resumed our trip. I look over, and there is Faith, trying to put one of the ice cubes into the soda bottle. 'Mom,' she said, 'this would be nice, if it fit.' I said, 'hunny, just pour it into the cup.'

"As I drove, it occurred to me, that this was how I was approaching the task of speaking here tonight. I was trying to make it fit, when in fact, it was much simpler than I was making it."

"It has been my experience in recovery that my higher power doesn't show me where I am going, but where I am. When I know that, when I am comfortable with that, then I am ready to move forward under her direction.

"So here I am." She raised her eyes briefly, "and you're still there."

Laughter. Then silence.

"I was born and raised in a little town called Silver Lake. For those of you who are not familiar with that, it's about 60 miles west of the Lakeview Metropolitan Area."

Laughter.

"Yea. I'm a hillbilly. There were six children born into my family. Two older step-brothers, a younger sister, and two younger brothers. I am not sure what to say about my birth family.

"My birth family had this escapist vision of what life could be like if they removed all the social confines from their daily lives, and lived...naturally. Without electricity....running water......plumbing.

"Last week at my Women's soul Meeting, a sister referred to herself as running around like a chicken with its head cut off. Believe me, no matter how busy you are, that could not be true. I've seen chickens in that most disturbing situation. I wouldn't describe it as natural.

"Several childhood experiences have impacted my thinking, my using, and my recovery. These are the core issues I have gathered and carried with me on my journey."

"The first is my relationship with my stepbrother. He was six years older then me, and as mean as the Devil. He reminded me everyday that he lived to hurt me. When I was 6, and he was 12, I let him molest me, in exchange for a trinket. A music box... wow! What a deal!"

Laughter from an audience who knew about being used.

"The experience was the beginning of a hundred experiences that were painful and ugly. Most important though, were the consequences. First, I told my mother, and after some thought, she said, 'Punk, don't let him do that again.'

"The second consequence to the experience was the creation of an individual in my mind who took over the job of protecting me. She talked to me frequently, guided me in my daily safety decisions, and got mad when I hurt. If you were a child of abuse or neglect, and reach back in time and take a really good look, you may find you had a guardian of your own."

She paused; the room was ever so quiet. Not looking up, Lena continued.

"I started drinking when I was quite young. I remember feeling joy for the first time when I found a beer and drank it.

"Like many families who set out on a philosophical journey, my parents did not reach their destination. Their ship sank, so to speak. My father disappeared into that place that deadbeat dads go, my mother moved us into a small town, and began the process of living again. It was a culture shock, and a confusing time for the six of us. All of us dealt with it in different ways, and I can only tell my story. But, just know, there was enough suffering to go around. My siblings have had just as many struggles as I have.

"When I was twelve, I began to choose my friends by the size of their parents' liquor supply. I not only consumed their alcohol, but I managed to take some for later. I was a wise-ass, foul mouth, and snotty little tomboy. Most of all, I was pissed off. It wasn't long before I went to live in deadbeat dad land, with my deadbeat dad. (Yeah, I still have issues with that)

"I was gone one year, and when I returned to Oregon, I was a pregnant 15 year old with a drinking problem. After an abortion, I gave up living with my birth family forever.

"I lived in the streets of Barberton for a summer, until the police raided a drug house and found me in one of the closets. At that point, I had two distinct behaviors: scared girl, and raging bitch. The only thing that made life comfortable was alcohol. Unfortunately, fifteen-year-old girls do not have trouble getting that.

"Children services placed me at a youth ranch, and then a foster home. I was a good learner. The youth ranch experience, and the consistency of a foster home, kept me alive for the rest of my teen years.

"When I was seventeen I found my mission in life. I was going to punish my parents for being the ugly hurtful people they were, by having a family of my own, and showing them how irresponsible they were. Hey, I was seventeen. I thought having a family of my own would make me a valuable person.

"One week after my eighteenth birthday, I married my best friend, you know that person who is over twenty-one and can buy for you."

The audience laughed at the clear confession of manipulation in her own set up to failure.

"He had seen me through a lot of situations, and proven his loyalty, which is very important to us unmanageable types. I was still suffering, but my inner turmoil was more or less under control with the use of alcohol.

"I could not see far enough into the future, to ask myself what I was going to do when I turned 21 and could buy my own consumption. Come on, that was three years away!"

Laughter.

"For twelve years I lived and worked as a functioning alcoholic. I had two baby girls that I loved dearly, every day. I had a doormat for a husband that I walked on every day. Life was good. It was an American dream."

Laughter.

"Until I turned twenty-eight. I looked at myself really hard, and knew I had been lying. I was so miserable, and I was making my family so miserable, that I did the unthinkable. I took an inventory. As difficult as that was to look at, it changed my life. This is what I found in my inventory.

"I was dependant on alcohol everyday. I weighted 198 lbs. Beer and cookies for breakfast will do that to a person."

Laughter. She continued, slowly and quietly, with her story.

"I had 14 jobs that year, quitting each one for a different reason. I had little formal education. I thought everyone was better than me; but pretended I was a queen of all that is good, and keeper of special knowledge."

Lena laughed quietly with the audience.

"I had no money or property of my own. I had two daughters who wanted and needed me to parent them. I had a husband that needed as much direction and attention as the children. I did have one close friend though; Oprah, she came over every afternoon at four."

Laughter.

"I had a flat religious experience, with no spiritual value. I wanted to die."

Lena paused then went on.

"I couldn't think or sleep without consuming alcohol first. I had a husband who liked to have sex with me when I was passed out cold. Apparently, I didn't struggle as much."

Laughter. Lena's self-effacing humor was natural. She didn't want to hide or hold back anything. Her tone continued low and slow, as she concentrated on the story.

"Seeing those items on paper was overwhelming. I cried the most refreshing cry I have ever had. That inventory pretty much spelled out my life. I read it over and over until I knew it by heart. Sobbing, I burned it in the fireplace. This was not a spiritual activity. I was ashamed and afraid someone would find it. No one was to know. Except God. I needed God."

She paused. "I came to a conclusion that day. I saw two options. Try out for the Jerry Springer show, or get sober and do life differently.

"For the first time in my life I prayed. I blamed my addiction to alcohol as the reason for all my problems. I asked for sobriety. But then I drank again, and again I begged God for sobriety. I asked from an unknown God to, 'take this obsession from me, or give me the courage to hang myself off the balcony.' Death was my only back up plan.

"To my amazement, it worked. I got sober. I found a new obsession: change. I became obsessed with losing weight and getting an education. I continued my one-sided relationship with Oprah. I watched her faithfully and I stopped eating. I went 28 days with nothing but diet coke and coffee. I lost 30 pounds. Then I went an additional six months on nothing but a bagel a day, sometimes less. I was just as obsessed with losing weight as I had been with drinking. I believed being thin would make me a valuable person.

"Consistently compulsive, I attained an education in the same obsessive way. I enrolled in the university, and I took five classes a term. I was just as obsessed with education as I was with drinking. It was what I had to do at the time. I felt trapped by the life I had created. I was willing to do everything necessary to get out of it. I believed getting a college degree would make me a valuable person.

"What I got from an education was a bit of understanding. You see, the only four-year program that fit my schedule was in economics, and economics just happens to be the foundation of all the principles our society is based on. It is an economic analysis that guides our conscious and unconscious, even our emotional decisions. An education provided me with the principles of how to understand a problem, and choose a solution that has the most benefit for the least cost. Sounds simple? It isn't. Because I first needed to understand myself, before I could understand what to do. Back to recovery I had to go."

Slowly, methodically, Lena pulled herself back into her past.

"When you change yourself, it has effects on the rest of your family. I had been a pretty good stay-at-home mom and alcoholic. I thought, in my most infantile wisdom, that I could be sober, and it would not affect my family in a negative way.

"My husband of those years was a drinking man. Not a lot, but who was I to judge? After my initial detoxification process, where I couldn't be near it, I felt he should have the freedom to drink again. After all, who was I to dictate someone else's life? So after six months of sobriety, my husband started drinking. What was surprising was that I resented him for it. I knew so little about myself that I encouraged my husband to choose something I would resent.

"Those first two years of recovery are kind of typical. I have heard a lot of addicts and alcoholics say that they thought it was just the___, you fill in the blank. See, I knew I was alcoholic, and I believed my life was unmanageable because of the alcohol.

I did not understand that it was me, not the alcohol that created the unmanageability. That's not to say that I didn't need to stop drinking. It was obvious not using or drinking was a necessary first step to recovery. I realized though, that for the kind of joy and peace I wanted to experience, it couldn't be the only step.

"Well, a person cannot hang onto the side of a cliff forever. That's what sobriety was like for me. One slip away from falling. When a family situation arose that I could not deal with, I drank again. I had to drink again.

"For a while, a month or so, it helped. Then life started getting out of control again. I was driving drunk. I stopped going to my classes. I began looking for a more intense drug, because alcohol was very toxic, and well, I didn't want to get fat again. Sadly, most of my self worth came from my appearance at that time.

"We don't get to choose our epiphany experience. The last day I was loaded, I had an epiphany experience. I acted out selfishly, destructively, and it hit me, that I had to be willing to change everything, if I wanted to live without getting loaded. I had to choose.

"When I woke up the next morning, I was done with drinking. I had spent two years sober, working on nothing but abstinence. I went to a meeting and shared that nothing had changed except I took up less space in a room, and I knew how to balance my checkbook. Those two reasons were not enough to stay sober. I got up that day, and became willing. Willing to do whatever it took to find a new way of life, in thinking, and in doing, so that I never had to take another drink.

"One of the biggest changes came when I allowed my guardian, Ellen, to leave. She was a crazy mean voice in my head, and I became willing to allow God to be my guardian. When I came to believe that a power greater then I, and Ellen, could restore me to sanity, I let go of Ellen.

"I faced for the first time in my life, living and caring for myself. It was exciting and frightening at the same time. I remember going to meetings and sharing how afraid I was. But, there was real excitement as well. I just wasn't going to cop to it, because, well, if I crashed and burned, it would have been a bad call, you know?

"I took the kids and moved out on my own and began working at a bank. I had some help with the kids, but honestly, the schedule was difficult. My life was working and going to meetings, and doing things with the kids. Life offered many subjects to work the steps on, because, well, life is tough to relate to. At least it was for me.

"For me, working the steps is kinda like vomiting."

The audience laughed nervously. The steps are sacred.

"First, you don't look forward to it. Any one here like to vomit?"

Nervous laughter.

"Just like vomiting, I'm not in charge of when it's time. When I'm nauseous the first thing I do is get real still and quiet, trying to postpone the inevitable. Even though I know I will feel better. Writing my fourth step... well, let's face it, working every step, is much like that. But when I need to do it, the urgency will drive me to doing it.

"Yea. Just like vomiting, working the steps can be messy. All sorts of stuff comes up. Stuff I have crammed down so far, I was sure it would never see the light of consciousness. But, like vomiting, postponing working the steps won't help. However, using the correct receptacle will. You see, writing during the process can be more effective then verbally spewing unprocessed garbage onto your coworkers or family members. Oh, they will remember it, and you will be sorry."

Laughter and applause.

"Of course, the point is to feel better. But that is only on the surface. Internally, garbage I had kept bottled up inside me has been removed. I then can choose whether I am going to take that garbage back, or consume some additional garbage, probably of the same variety, because I am committed to the same stupid stuff.

"Yea. You know you're a hillbilly when you use vomiting as an analogy for the spiritual process of healing."

Laughter, then silence. Lena didn't want to shortchange the formal process of recovery by reducing it to a comedic metaphor.

"To give credit where it belongs, I did, and still do, practice the steps of the program, in the order they are written. This is what I have done in order to become more comfortable with who I am." Lena paused and held up her index finger.

"First, I admitted that I was addicted to alcohol, and could not change my behavior on my own." Lena held up her second finger. She straightened her shoulders and looked up at the audience.

"Second, I took the risk of hope, that a power greater then myself, could do for me that which I could not do for myself. I had tried everything I could think of to quit drinking, and only achieved making my life worse of a mess. Only after I admitted defeat, could I risk hoping their was something else that could do for me what I could not do for myself."

Lena held up her third finger. With strength in her voice, she held up her head.

"Third. I went forward on faith that there was a God. I started behaving *as if* there is a God, instead of behaving as if there weren't." With a new strength in her voice, Lena held up her next finger.

"Fourth, I looked at myself in the mirror: honestly, humbly, and with a compassionate *God of my understanding*. The gift from looking at myself is that I found an abundance of love and compassionate, as well as fear, greed, envy and self-centeredness.

"Fifth, " Lena said steadily, holding up all her fingers and her thumb, thrusting her hand open toward the crowd, "I shared my most inner secrets with another person. You know, they say you are only as sick as your secrets.

"Sixth, I willingly participated in *what* I do and *how* I do, my life. I no longer live with a default system that baffles me. I no longer can say, 'I don't know why' I did this or that. I know why, because I play an active role in my life." Lena paused before she went on.

"Seven, I humbly asked God, my higher power, to remove those items from my garden that were not compatible with sobriety. Eight, with the help of my sponsor, and with the strength found in my new relationships, I looked at the wreckage of my past. I looked at those decisions I made carelessly. I looked at the anger and pain I caused in the lives of others.

Lena's voice began to sound tired. She sighed and dropped her extended hand. "Nine, I began to mend my garden by filling in the holes, cleaning up the trash, and apologizing for the unexplainable mess I had made. Ten, I continued to watch for the behavior that puts my sobriety at risk.

"Eleven, I continue to go to God, my higher power, for direction and guidance. Because…its not just about cleaning up my life…its also about getting new direction and guidance for *today*."

"Twelve, I placed myself in service to the program of recovery, and my community at large both personally and professionally." Lena paused for a moment, wondering what to say next. The silent audience gave no hint of restlessness.

"When I first came into recovery, I thought the steps of recovery sounded like a formula that had nothing to do with *real* life. I became acutely aware of my need to work the steps on real life problems when I began working.

"You see for me, working full time in a professional environment gave this hillbilly girl from Silver Lake a lot of topics to work the steps on. My most tenacious character defect, honesty, was always there to be practiced. That's what it came down to for me. Understanding and acknowledging my problems with life, and then choosing to practice life with the solution given to me by my higher power, or continue with perfecting the problem.

"When I came back to the program after relapse, one of my biggest issues was the God As A Man, concept. I was searching for an authentic female self, and I was having trouble communicating with the Man God. I was told in this program, that if you cannot communicate, or humble yourself, to a power greater then yourself, you ask for help. So I asked for help. And God answered me, through another person in recovery.

"I went to a convention my first year, and a woman in recovery was telling her story. When she came to the part about God, she said, 'If you have a problem with God, talk to his mother.' For me, that was what I needed to hear. I could get on my knees, and go to a spiritual garden, and receive communication from the mother God. I could, and I did. Most important though, was that it worked.

"When I am afraid, when I know change has arrived and life is asking something new from me, I find comfort in prayer. I can and do, close my eyes, and find myself in the most pleasant of surroundings, with a higher power that knows and loves me. I trust her wisdom, and find relief in her guidance.

"The myth that employment and recovery are not compatible is a lie. I know. I've had to work on this issue everyday. It does get better, for any of you that face the same thing.

"My last year of getting loaded I had fourteen different jobs. I was a mess. I couldn't seem to show up, and when I did, I had a problem staying for any amount of time. When I did stay, my skin would crawl with anxiety, and I would have panic attacks.

"Yeah, I would say this qualifies as an issue. The one positive thing I found in my inventory of employment was that I really do value work. I really do want to work and participate in life. So after relapse, when I had about three months of sobriety, I began working at a bank. It was really nice. Everyone was polite. The women I worked with were beautiful. I got to practice showing up on time, dressing in nice clothes, and talking to people in shallow superficial polite conversations. My boss was nice. My coworkers were lovely."

Lena paused. "It was very difficult. I couldn't handle it. Everyday I wanted to quit. Everyday I felt uncomfortable. But growth doesn't come from doing the easy stuff. Growth comes from showing up and doing the uncomfortable things that challenge you.

"After two and a half years, I quit. In my infant wisdom, I felt I needed a new environment. It was a foolish and rash decision. I became desperate for money, so what did I do? I went to work at another bank. This time I was determined to be more authentic. But my authentic person didn't fit the corporate mold. Yeah, you can guess what happened. They fired my ass."

Laughter.

"The fact was… I was sober, but still very lost. I remember crying, and then going to bed. I stayed in bed for six months. Then one day, I got up and got ready for work again. Eventually, getting ready for work paid off.

"Today, I work with people who face a huge monster in their lives. I work with people who have been discriminated against because of HIV. They truly have a unique perspective, and I value the work a great deal. I have continued to search for an authentic self, but I am aware that I must make some adjustments in order to perform my duty to my employer.

"The gifts of recovery are huge. That inventory list I took six short years ago is only ashes now. I have a bit of health, I can think and sleep without chemical assistance. I have children who love and respect me, and a support group I can perform service work in. If none of this were so, I would still be here though, because it is the gift of a higher power that has made the biggest difference in my life. I can and did take my most difficult issue to her, and she did reveal a solution. That issue was Ellen. Ellen was a guardian for a young child. When I replaced her with my higher power, she disappeared. But I missed her.

"My higher power said that it is best to be whole, even if fractured. So with that in mind, I moved Ellen from death to distraction, from the guardian who leapt to her death because she had been replaced by a higher power, to my eternal narrator. She is perfect for the job, because she talks all the time. Narration does not involve guidance, and she does not give direction in my life. So, for the first time, I have a sense of wholeness. That is a gift.

"I do not know what the future is going to bring. I do not know if it will require more courage than I have, or if my future is almost over. The seasons show me the wonder of God's plan. Even if that means the wind changes my life. That's the difference in me today. Through recovery I have learned that I am no more in control of my life then I am of the wind. I can hide from it, but I cannot control it. Today I choose not to hide in a small life of my own creation. Today I can allow the natural world of God's design, to leave its mark on me."

"We all come to recovery with a specific goal in mind. When I first came to recovery, I wanted to become a lesbian and hike the Himalayas."

Laughter.

"In a way, that has happened." She paused. "Not literally, of course."

Laughter.

"See, I did find a woman to love. I have found a bit of myself..." She paused again, thinking. "And I am on a spiritual journey, with all the beauty and raw scenery one would expect from a steep climb. My guide has patience and encouragement, having traveled this path many times before.

"God's will for me is to come to believe. God's plan for me is everything between birth and death. All the dark experiences and all the light experiences are woven together with others like yourselves, who are on the same journey. That fabric, made up of 'coming to believe' experiences provides my life with warmth and comfort… color and pattern. For this I am deeply grateful.

"I know that there is more to recovery than I have revealed tonight. But I have yet to experience it. Just for today, that is all I have to share."

"Thank you."

The crowd jumped to its feet with applause and cheering. Dazed, Lena tried to walk toward Michael's table. People were grabbing her and hugging her, all trying to speak at once. The chairperson was at the microphone, calling everyone to form a circle to close the meeting. As soon as they closed, Lena withdrew to the motor home. She just wanted to be alone.

Michael entered the darkened motor home. He found Lena sitting on the edge of the bed in the very back. She was looking out the window at the darkening sky.

"Hi girl," he said and sat down on the bed beside her.

"Hi."

"What can I do for you?" Michael asked quietly in the dark.

"Marry me."

"Okay," he said, as if she had requested a glass of water. "But…"

"But what?" Lena asked defensively.

"But we are already married," Michael said.

"I know." Lena lay down on her side, facing the window. "Its just that...now I'm ready." Michael lay down behind her and gently curved his body around hers. They lay together and watched the fireworks begin. They had the rest of their lives ahead of them. They were in no hurry for this.

So I will wait. I wait to see what Lena will do next. She had attained that American Dream of home, family, and educational status. Is she so simple as to resign herself to acquiring more of the same? More house, more car, more status, more items. If this American Dream is based on acquisition and consumption, are individuals ever allowed to have enough? What would they do if that happened?

As for me, I was born out of a child's desperation. I have been incarcerated on this planet for the crime of coming to the aid of a small child in a hillbilly town in that great state of Oregon. As if that were not bad enough, I was evicted as the guardian, with all those privileges and power, and reassigned as a narrator for a poorly funded, never ending production.

So I write. I narrate all those indecent developments that Lena seems to produce just by showing up for her life. I write in my most stubborn manner, about the ridiculous nature of the American pursuits, not because they provide meaning or are of any significance, but because they are an indication of how little I am missing by being ensnared in the life of a woman who will always be a shabby little girl. I write for *that girl* who surrendered her life in the established, who wanders painfully in the fringe for the chance to view the unexpected and the less obvious. I narrate for *that girl* who has found love in a modest corner of life.

As for the fringe, what can I say? Either you understand or you don't. Lena was a product of a fringe family, married to achieve membership into the main fabric, and left those comforts to be unhappy, poor, yet sober, woman in the fringe. Is the fringe good or bad? Does the fringe even exist outside of this narration? I don't know. Just remember: Rain is wet, fire is hot, and nothing is real until it is personal.